Sara didn't need a map to know she was in big-time trouble.

In challenging Jake Dawson so blatantly for the Three-Stars ranch, she had clearly wandered onto dangerous turf.

She dared a peek at the man while he slept. The raw masculinity that greeted her gaze took her breath away.

She'd seen the rippling muscles in his shoulders and arms as he worked bare chested. But the combined effect of tapered waist, lean hips, powerful legs and…and, well! It all slammed through her like a runaway locomotive.

She wanted him with a hunger that stunned her.

But if she wasn't careful, this consuming need could cloud her thinking. And she needed all her wits about her if she was going to hang on to the ranch.

That was her number-one priority.

Wasn't it?

Dear Reader,

Happy Valentine's Day! Love is in the air, and Special Edition has plenty of little cupids to help matchmake! There are family stories here, there are breathtaking romances there—you name it, you'll find love in each and every Silhouette Special Edition.

This month we're pleased to welcome new-to-Silhouette author Angela Benson. Her debut book for Special Edition, *A Family Wedding*, is a warm, wonderful tale of friends falling in love…and a darling little girl's dream come true.

We're also proud to present Jane Toombs's dramatic tale, *Nobody's Baby*, our THAT'S MY BABY! title. Jane also has written under the pseudonym Diana Stuart, and this is her first book for Special Edition under her real name. And speaking of firsts, please welcome to Special Edition, veteran Silhouette Desire author Peggy Moreland, by reading *Rugrats and Rawhide*—a tender tale of love for this Valentine's month.

Sherryl Woods returns with a marvelous new series— THE BRIDAL PATH. Don't miss the first book, *A Ranch for Sara*, a rollicking, heartwarming love story. The second and third titles will be available in March and April! And the Valentine's Day thermostat continues to rise with Gina Wilkins's sparkling tale of opposites attracting in *The Father Next Door*.

Finally, Natalie Bishop presents readers with the perfect February title—*Valentine's Child*. This tale of love lost and then rediscovered is full of the Valentine's Day spirit!

I hope you enjoy this book, and each and every title to come!

Sincerely,

Tara Gavin, Senior Editor

Please address questions and book requests to:
Silhouette Reader Service
U.S.: 3010 Walden Ave., P.O. Box 1325, Buffalo, NY 14269
Canadian: P.O. Box 609, Fort Erie, Ont. L2A 5X3

SHERRYL WOODS

A RANCH FOR SARA

Silhouette ®

SPECIAL ▼ EDITION ®

Published by Silhouette Books
America's Publisher of Contemporary Romance

For Kim and Jay, in honor of their walk down the
bridal path, with love and good wishes for a long and
happy life together.

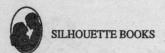 SILHOUETTE BOOKS

ISBN 0-373-24083-X

A RANCH FOR SARA

Books by Sherryl Woods

SHERRYL WOODS

lives by the ocean, which, she says, provides daily inspiration for the romance in her soul. She further explains that her years as a television critic taught her about steamy plots and humor; her years as a travel editor took her to exotic locations; and her years as a crummy weekend tennis player taught her to stick with what she enjoyed most—writing. "What better way is there," Sherryl asks, "to combine all that experience than by creating romantic stories?" Sherryl loves to hear from her readers. You may write to her at P.O. Box 490326, Key Biscayne, FL 33149. A self-addressed, stamped envelope is appreciated for a reply.

Trent Wilde
requests the pleasure
of your company
at the wedding of his daughter

Miss Sara Wilde

to

Mr. Jake Dawson

A humdinger of a hoedown
to follow at their ranch!

Chapter One

It was the moment Jake Dawson had been waiting for for ten long years, maybe for his whole life. Three-Stars Ranch was going to be his, every beautiful, rugged acre of it, every head of cattle.

He surreptitiously surveyed his immediate surroundings. He would even own this magnificent old house with its stone fireplaces, high-beamed ceilings and gleaming wide-planked wood floors. It was a home a man could take pride in, a home in which the richest and most powerful could be entertained without shame.

It was a hell of a long way from a two-room shack that hadn't had electricity half the time. Almost every paltry cent his father had earned back then—on those rare occasions when he worked at all—had been spent on booze. Food had ranked a distant second.

Electricity and a telephone had been treated as luxuries.

"You won't regret selling Three-Stars to me," he promised Trent Wilde, the man who'd given him a chance when he'd come off the rodeo circuit, broken and battered by one too many championship bull rides.

"See that I don't," Trent said.

The sharp words were tempered with the same sort of gruff affection that had always made Jake feel more like a son than an employee. Their unexpected rapport was something Jake treasured. Trent Wilde was one of the few people on earth he trusted and respected, one of even fewer he could honestly say he cared about.

Not that they hadn't had their run-ins through the years. They both had arrogance and stubborn pride to spare. On top of that, Jake had been bitter when his rodeo career had ended so abruptly. The rodeo circuit had been his ticket out of poverty. Losing it to an avoidable injury had cost him his hard-won self-esteem. No rodeo rider would have allowed a stupid distraction over a woman to cause him to forget to check every piece of equipment before a ride.

He'd taken his own stupidity out on anyone who tried to get too close. He'd had a chip on his shoulder the size of all Wyoming. Wisely, Trent hadn't knocked it off. He'd nudged at it, patiently and persistently, until Jake had had no choice but to settle down and grow up, something he'd mistakenly thought he'd already done during those hard years at home.

"I have faith in you," Trent continued now, pouring them both a celebratory snifter of his best brandy. "You've worked hard and earned every break I've given you. You'll be able to take Three-Stars into the next century, make it the ranch I always dreamed it could be."

Given the fact that Three-Stars was one of the biggest, most profitable ranches in the state, the older man's faith might have been daunting, but Jake had been chomping at the bit for this chance for years now. When Trent had first broached the subject of his buying Three-Stars, Jake had thought it would take longer. No one had expected Trent to retire this soon.

But ever since the older man had been widowed two years earlier, it seemed the spirit had gone out of him. He was anxious to get away and try new things, he'd told Jake. He wanted to kick up his heels a bit, whatever the devil that meant to a man nearing sixty. He declared he'd earned it.

"Have you spoken to your daughters about this?" Jake asked warily, thinking of the three willful young women who'd given Trent Wilde fits during their teens. Since their mother's death, each was more protective of their father than the other. None were likely to take the news that he was abandoning them and the ranch lightly.

Trent shrugged. "They'll hear about my plans when the time is right," he said. "I don't want them fussing over me, thinking maybe I've gone round the bend just because I want to get away from this place and soak up a little sun." He lit up one of the imported cigars he favored and winked at Jake. "Maybe I'll just wait and drop 'em a note when I get to Arizona."

The answer was a little too evasive, a little too flip for Jake's satisfaction. He didn't like the idea of being left behind to explain things, a tactic Trent was perfectly capable of using to avoid argument. Danielle, Sara and Ashley Wilde were not exactly shrinking violets about making their opinions known. If any one of them disapproved of Trent's plans for the ranch, they could make the old man's life hell.

Not that they could change his mind, Jake admitted dryly.

The trouble was, once they'd given up on their father, they were more than likely to turn on Jake. He shuddered at the thought of coping with the monumental temper tantrums and devious manipulations of which they were capable. Jake considered whether any of them cared enough about Three-Stars to pitch a royal fit or to make serious trouble for him.

Dark-haired, dark-eyed Danielle, the oldest, appeared to be content enough living in town. Nearing thirty and thoroughly independent, she'd built a tidy little business for herself with her homemade jams and baked goods. She turned up at Three-Stars only for the command performances—Sunday dinner and holidays. Practical and sensible, she would cluck and worry over her father's decision, but she would probably go along with it, Jake concluded.

Ashley, the flirtatious blond beauty, had done half a dozen magazine covers since she'd moved to New York. Trent had them all proudly displayed on the wall behind him. With her modeling career in high gear, Jake couldn't imagine her caring one way or the other if the ranch were sold. Other than the sad trip to attend her mother's funeral, she hadn't even been home for a visit since she'd left. She'd made it plain that Riverton, Wyoming was the last place on earth she wanted to be.

Then there was Sara, a fiery, redheaded tomboy, whose reckless antics had nearly given her father apoplexy on more than one occasion. Something told Jake if there was going to be trouble, that was the quarter it would come from.

Sara had been dogging his footsteps, poking her nose into ranch business, asking questions, ever since he'd turned up on the ranch. He doubted there was a chore around the place she couldn't handle or a ranch hand she couldn't charm into doing exactly what she wanted. He wondered if his boss knew that. Like it or not, he'd better know now what Sara's reaction was likely to be. Jake never ran from a fight, but he sure liked to know when one was heading his way.

"What about Sara?" he asked bluntly.

Trent regarded him blankly. "What about her?"

Jake thought carefully about the best way to phrase his concerns without costing himself his dream. He settled for suggesting, "She seems to love the ranch."

"Well, of course, she does. It's her home," Trent said with the confidence of a man used to controlling his world and everyone in it. He paused, his expression suddenly nostalgic. "Nobody'll walk away from this place without regrets, not even me."

Before Jake could work up the courage to point out that maybe that meant he shouldn't sell, at least not yet, Trent was going on.

"As for Sara, she'll find someone she wants to marry one day soon. There are already half a dozen men who'd court her, if she'd give 'em a second look. I have one or two in mind. I'm thinking I'll give her a push before I leave. She'll settle down, have her own home, give me some grandbabies, same as the other two will eventually. Where would that leave Three-Stars? It would have been different if I'd had sons, but with daughters..."

Jake didn't bother pointing out that Trent's chauvinistic attitude was out of step with the times.

Trent shook his head sadly. "No, this is the best decision for all concerned. Besides, I made you a promise when you came here and I keep my promises. Now that I know for certain that this is still what you want, I'll have the lawyer here tomorrow to finalize the details and get busy with the paperwork. The bank won't be any problem. We'll close on the deal in no time and we can both get on about the business of living the rest of our lives the way we want."

Because he wanted desperately to believe it could be as simple as that, Jake pushed aside his worry over Sara's reaction and allowed himself to savor the moment. This time tomorrow Three-Stars would be all but his.

And once those papers were signed, no one on God's earth would ever steal it away from him.

Sara Wilde stood outside her father's office blatantly eavesdropping on his conversation with Jake Dawson. Seething with resentment, her temper rose with each traitorous word they spoke. Give him some grandbabies indeed! Hell would freeze over before she would do anything her father wanted ever again. The days of struggling to please him, to impress upon him how much alike they were, were over.

How could he sell Three-Stars, the only home Sara and her sisters had ever known? Just because they weren't boys! It just proved what she'd believed all along, that he'd named the ranch Three-Stars when he'd been anticipating three brilliant males to carry on the family name. She was surprised he hadn't taken down the sign over the gate and renamed the place once he'd realized there would be no sons. Maybe Three Little Flowers, she thought irritably.

What the heck did gender have to do with anything? By her teens she had developed a clear vision of what she wanted from life—to be as successful and powerful as her father, to take over Three-Stars. She'd known that both Dani and Ashley would give their blessing to the plan, but that vision had obviously never coincided with her old-fashioned daddy's views on the subject.

As his comments had just indicated, Trent Wilde would have turned her into a docile lady, content to be baking pies and making jams for some man. That sort of thing might be fine for Dani, but Sara had

ranching in her blood. In her view, running Three-
Stars Ranch was not only the most logical career
choice she could make, but more importantly, it was
her birthright. Had she been a son, as her father had
just so clearly stated, there would have been no question about it. Knowing that truly grated on her fem-
inist nature.

She knew as much about running the place as any
man on it, her father and Jake Dawson included. She
might have come away from college with the liberal
arts degree her father had thought suitable, but she'd
slipped in every agriculture and animal husbandry
course she could manage. She'd borrowed every
ranching book in her father's library at one time or
another and sneaked away to read them where he
wasn't likely to catch her. No one could have been
more prepared to take over Three-Stars than she was.
If he'd listened to even half her comments at the
dinner table, he would have known that.

How could her father sell the ranch to an outsider,
anyway? Not that Jake Dawson was exactly a
stranger. He'd been working for her father for ten
years, the past five of them as foreman.

Jake was bullheaded, condescending and every bit
as old-fashioned when it came to women as Trent
Wilde himself. In Sara's opinion that was a thorough
waste of one incredibly sexy, gorgeous hunk of man.

Thinking about Jake's easy-to-look-at features, his
thick, indecently touchable sun-streaked hair and
well-toned muscles distracted Sara from the crisis at
hand for several minutes. Woolgathering was one of
her worst habits, according to her critical father, who

was much more likely to find faults than virtues in his offspring. Daydreaming about the mysterious, un-attainable Jake was something she'd been doing for years. By now it was an impossible-to-shake habit.

Not that Jake had ever shown a lick of interest in her. He was polite and distant, answering her questions with the kind of aloof professionalism that would drive any woman who wanted to be noticed to distraction.

Used to getting her share of masculine attention, there had been times when Sara had been sorely tempted to strip naked and ride bareback through the fields just to see if she could stir a reaction out of him. Only the fear that she might not had kept her from trying it. If he merely tossed her a blanket in that cool, unflappable way of his, she'd never get over the humiliation.

Okay, so she was woolgathering again. It might be a fault under ordinary circumstances, she conceded, but not this time. She needed to find a way to thwart this deal and she needed to come up with it fast.

As the middle daughter in a family of strong-willed individuals, twenty-seven-year-old Sara had learned early to stake her claim on the things that mattered to her. She was as stubborn as her father's prize bull, a trait she'd inherited from a master.

Since there was no way to appeal to her father once his mind was made up, that left Jake. Fortu-nately, during the years Jake had been at Three-Stars, Sara had been observing him closely, more closely than was proper no doubt. She knew his strengths and weaknesses almost as well as she knew her own.

Jake was proud and smart and determined. He also had a tendency to enjoy a hand of poker every now and again, an occasional bet on football. That knowledge brought her the first smile she'd been able to muster since she'd overheard her father making that traitorous deal.

As any rodeo star had to be, Jake Dawson was a gambling man. And, as her father repeatedly said with despair, she was quite a risk taker herself.

If there was no way to convince her father to put her in charge of Three-Stars, then she'd just have to concentrate on making Jake change his mind about buying the spread. By the time her father and Jake were toasting their deal, she was pretty sure she had exactly the right scheme in mind, one that would appeal to the ex–rodeo champ's sense of danger and daring.

She ignored the possibility that trying to best a man as unpredictable as Jake might also get her into more trouble than she'd ever bargained for.

With the lawyer coming tomorrow, there was absolutely no time to waste weighing other options. She figured she had another half hour, while Jake and her father dawdled over that outrageously expensive brandy, to get ready. When Jake got back to his quarters, she would be waiting for him...with an offer he couldn't refuse.

Years of yearning for something of his own, something real and permanent were almost over, Jake thought as he paused to stare out over the rugged terrain after his meeting with Trent.

Spring hadn't yet made its way into Wyoming. The night air was crisp and clear. If he stared up at the sky, he could see a million stars, but he was more interested in what lay beneath, the land that was almost his. The stars might fuel a man's dreams, but it was land that gave him independence.

Ignoring his recent pledge to quit smoking, he shook a cigarette loose from the pack in his pocket, cupped his hand against the breeze and lit up. Something that felt an awful lot like contentment shimmered through him.

He had to stop himself from looking on this deal with Trent as some sort of a gift, something he didn't deserve. He'd worked damned hard to make it happen. He'd almost lost his chance because of a woman. Until that ill-fated romance, he'd saved darned near every penny he'd made on the rodeo circuit and most of his salary since he'd been at Three-Stars so he'd be ready when this day came. With the money he had to put down, no bank would be able to declare him a credit risk. Not that the Riverton Bank would dare to stand in the way of any deal Trent Wilde cared to make. Trent's deposits probably doubled those of everybody else in the area combined.

As far back as he could remember, Jake had had a single goal for his life: to own something, something no man could take away. He wasn't going to be satisfied with some little bungalow in town, either. Or starting from scratch with a few acres and a handful of cows. He wanted the biggest and best spread in the state, a place that would prove once and for all that Jake Dawson was somebody.

What happened tomorrow would be just the beginning, he promised himself as he stubbed out his cigarette and headed for home.

As he approached the three-room house that had been his since he came to work on the ranch, he noticed smoke curling from the chimney and a faint glow from inside that suggested someone had lit a fire. The sight stopped him in his tracks. What the hell was going on?

He slowed his approach and detoured to the north, which would give him a clearer view inside without making him readily visible to anyone watching the front walkway for him. Not that whoever was inside was exactly hiding the fact. Only a fool would light a fire while waiting to ambush someone.

Slipping up against the side of the house, he peeked in a window and instantly drew in a sharp breath. To his astonishment, Sara Wilde was curled up in his easy chair in front of the fire.

Her hair, which she normally wore twisted into some sort of knot on top of her head or tucked into a Stetson, waved down past her shoulders. The red shimmered with golden lights.

She was wearing a silky, soft green blouse the shade of moss that dipped and clung in all the right places. Her long, slender legs were encased in form-fitting denim. Her feet were bare, the toenails an unexpected and very feminine sizzling pink.

The sight was enough to make stronger men than

Jake weak with desire. Out-of-the-blue lust slammed through him like a runaway freight train.

Every instinct he possessed told him he'd better proceed with caution. Sara wasn't in the habit of dropping by unannounced, much less taking up residence while he wasn't home. She looked like a woman with something on her mind, the same alarming, dangerous something Jake suddenly had on his.

He could cope with this without giving in to temptation, he swore to himself. He had to. He wasn't about to risk tomorrow's deal on a one-night fling with the boss's daughter, no matter how inviting the idea seemed right at this moment.

Besides, this was Sara, for God's sake. He'd watched her grow up. He'd never thought of her as anything more than a pesky kid sister. Okay, an *attractive* pesky kid sister, who was so far off-limits to a man like him, she might as well have been in Alaska.

After sucking in a final lungful of the crisp, night air, he strolled inside and tossed his hat in the direction of a rack on the wall. It caught and held. Sara's delicate eyebrows rose an approving fraction, but her gaze remained steady and unblinking. Jake's pulse bucked under that thoroughly feminine look. How had he missed the fact that little Sara had grown up? The daring she'd shown as a girl took on far more dangerous implications in the woman she'd become.

He shoved his hands in his pockets and rocked back on his booted heels. He cleared his throat and aimed for sounding casual. "So, what brings you by?"

"We need to talk."

"About?"

"The deal you're about to make with my father."

Jake grimaced. He'd guessed right. She was going to make trouble. It was written all over that pretty face of hers.

"I wasn't sure if you knew about it," he said cautiously.

A frown passed over her face. "I sure as heck didn't," she admitted heatedly. "Not until I overheard you and daddy talking tonight. Quite a secret, wouldn't you say?"

"Since you're here, I gather you don't approve."

"No," she said succinctly. "I don't."

"Then shouldn't you be talking to your father?"

"We both know that would be a waste of time."

Jake steeled himself against the hurt and fury he could read in her eyes. He couldn't afford to feel any sympathy under the circumstances.

"So is talking to me," he said tersely. "This is a business deal, pure and simple."

"Not to me, it isn't," she said. "We're talking about my home."

"Mine now," he retorted.

"Not quite," she contradicted. She stood up and moved slowly toward him. "Jake, you and I have always been friends, haven't we?"

Warning bells echoed in his head at the plaintive question. "Yes," he agreed warily.

Her gaze lifted and clashed with his. Why had he

never noticed that her eyes were precisely the shade of emeralds shot through with fire? He had to drag his gaze away, force himself to focus on something innocuous like the dishes still sitting in his sink.

"See," she said blithely. "We've already agreed on something. We're friends."

"Sweetheart, I'm not sure where you're going with this, but I surely do wish you'd get there."

"Okay, the bottom line is, I have a counteroffer I don't think you're going to be able to resist."

He swallowed hard at the soft, provocative tone. Sweet heaven, she was going to try to seduce the ranch away from him. Temptation curled through him, tangling his thoughts. Or maybe just seduce him, then scream bloody murder afterward so that Trent would chase him off with a shotgun. Either way, she represented danger.

"No way," he managed to mutter, backing up a step.

Her lush lips curved seductively. "You don't even know what I have in mind."

He couldn't lose sight of his goal, when it was so close. Not for this woman. Not for anyone. "Doesn't matter," he said vehemently. "I want Three-Stars."

"You want it badly, don't you?"

"More than you can imagine."

"I doubt that," she said wryly. "Remember, I want it, too."

"Which brings us to an impasse."

"Not necessarily."

She stepped so close he could smell the soft, spicy perfume she wore, something intoxicating and wicked. She slid her fingers up his chest until they were less than a hairsbreadth from the burning skin of his neck. Jake wondered if hell could possibly be any worse than this. To keep from reaching for her, he jammed his hands in his pockets so roughly that his knuckles scraped on denim.

"I think you and I could come..." she hesitated, then added "...to an arrangement."

"An arrangement," Jake repeated, his voice choked. Trouble was rapidly escalating into calamity.

She nodded and smiled. It was a look of such innocence that Jake's thoughts went spinning. What the devil was she up to?

"I want you to make a bet with me, Jake," she said sweetly.

"A bet," he echoed.

"An all-or-nothing bet," she elaborated.

He swallowed hard and tried to get his mind to focus on what she was saying. Too damned much was riding on this for him to be fuzzy headed and thinking with some part of his anatomy that clearly wasn't connected to his brain.

He deliberately backed up a step, then another. He figured he wouldn't be safely out of harm's way unless he fled the house completely, but he refused to do that. He just had to keep reminding himself that Sara was like a pesky little sister, not a seductive, alluring woman. Climbing Mount Everest would have been easier, he conceded, as his mouth went dry and his skin flushed.

"Exactly what is this bet you want me to make?" he asked. If the woman wanted to bet he couldn't go another minute resisting her, he might as well forget about the ranch. His body was carrying on an argument with his brain the likes of which no man should have to endure. His brain was losing, flat out shutting down while his senses raged.

She smiled once more and his knees went weak. She moved closer again. Her fingers crept along his neck and tunneled through his hair. This time he didn't seem to have the will to move away. It took pure grit to keep his hands in his pockets.

"It's simple really," she explained. "And the odds are all in your favor."

Jake seriously doubted that.

"After all, you were a rodeo champion, weren't you?" she added smoothly.

Jake's gaze narrowed. What did his rodeo victories have to do with anything? At some point in the last ten seconds this conversation had taken a twist he hadn't followed.

Sara stood on tiptoe, her lips so close he could feel her sweet breath fanning across his face. "You were good, weren't you?"

"Very good," Jake agreed.

"Then this shouldn't be any problem for you at all. In fact, I'm probably crazy for even bothering…" Her voice trailed off as if at this very moment she might be reconsidering the idea that had brought her to his house.

Yeah, he thought, she was crazy all right. Crazy like a fox. Those warning bells in his head were clanging loud enough to wake the dead. Every fiber of his being heeded the call to arms.

Jake untangled her hands from his hair and retreated another step, out of touching range, if not out of danger.

"You're going to have to spell it out, sweetheart. I'm afraid you've lost me."

She smiled. "It's not so complicated," she assured him. "I just want to challenge you to a bull-riding contest, winner take all."

Chapter Two

Jake stared openmouthed at the woman standing before him, hands on hips, fiery hair dancing around her face like dangerous flames caught by the wind.

He was absolutely certain he couldn't have heard Sara Wilde correctly. If she'd clobbered him over the head with a two-by-four, Jake couldn't have been any more flabbergasted. Was it truly possible that she was willing to risk her life on the back of a bull to get control of the ranch he'd just agreed to buy from her father? Surely not even Sara, who'd pulled some pretty outrageous stunts in her time, would suggest something so crazy.

"You want to do what?" he asked slowly.

"I want to challenge you to a bull-riding contest," she repeated every bit as calmly as she'd delivered the same incredible words the first time.

She had certainly dashed cold water on his libido, he thought wryly. This was a long way from the seduction he'd been convinced she had in mind. An unmistakable and worrisome sense of disappointment flitted through him. Either deliberately or inadvertently, Miss Sara Wilde had started something she clearly had no intention of finishing. He wondered if he'd ever be able to look at her in the same way again.

That, of course, begged the immediate problem: what to do about this absurd bet of hers. It was taking considerable effort to hold back the laughter threatening to bubble up from somewhere deep inside him. He hadn't had a good belly laugh in a long time. The glint in her eyes as she waited for an answer told him he didn't want to have one at her expense.

"Well?" she prodded, when he remained silent.

"You've obviously lost your mind," Jake said succinctly. "For starters, women don't ride bulls."

"Sure, they do. I've researched it."

"You've researched it," he repeated, then shook his head in disgust. "Well, that's just dandy."

To prove her point, she listed a whole string of women riders. Jake wasn't impressed.

"Maybe what I should have said was women don't ride bulls in competition with me."

Sara's willful expression never wavered. "You aren't chicken, are you?"

The deliberately taunting question had him gritting his teeth. "I was bull-riding champ on the circuit three years running," he reminded her. "If anyone ought to be quaking in their boots here, it's not me.

Forget it, sweet Sara. You're playing out of your league."

"You don't scare me," she insisted.

"I may not, but a thousand pounds or so of spitting-mad bull ought to give you pause," he suggested. She did lose a little color at that, but her eyes flashed with grim determination.

"Will you or won't you?" she demanded as if he hadn't already given her a straight answer.

Jake was realizing for the first time that Sara Wilde was the kind of irritating woman who heard only what she wanted to hear and kept needling until she got an answer twisted around to her way of thinking.

"I won't." He hoped the flat, unequivocal statement left absolutely no room for negotiation.

He regarded her curiously. "Where did you come up with such a screwball idea?" he asked, genuinely puzzled by the out-of-the-blue proposition. Women had been making outrageous and indecent offers to him since the day he won his first rodeo title, but not one of them had ever suggested trying to outride him on the back of a mean old bull.

Of course, Sara Wilde wasn't like most other women. He'd known that the moment he'd set eyes on her. She'd been barely seventeen back then and she'd had audacity to spare. To Jake's private amusement, not a single one of Trent Wilde's attempts to tame her had had any effect. Her sweet, ladylike mother had been totally flummoxed by her out-of-control daughter.

At one point, Trent had threatened to send Sara off to some fancy finishing school where she'd learn

manners and social graces. Sara had responded by
stealing a horse and hiding out in the wilderness for
an entire weekend on her own. Trent had been so
relieved when she'd sauntered back into the house
unharmed that he'd dropped the notion of sending
her away.

When she'd reluctantly gone off to a nice sedate
college, Trent had breathed a sigh of relief. He'd ev-
idently figured a few years in the world of academia
would accomplish what he hadn't been able to. At
the very least he'd been counting on her to make a
good match and become some other man's headache.
His bewildered expression when she'd returned
home, unchanged and unmarried, had kept Jake entertained for days.

Jake understood that kind of grit and determination
better than most. He had a willful streak of his own
that was a mile wide. It had served him well so far.
He won most arguments, whether he started them or
not.

But then again, like Trent, he'd never butted heads
with anyone quite like Sara before. Even now, she
was trying to stare him down, undaunted by his flat
refusals.

"I want Three-Stars," she said bluntly. "So do
you. There's only one way I can see to settle it. If I
stay on that bull longer than you, then the ranch is
mine. You back off and tell Daddy you have other
plans for the rest of your life. Go steal somebody
else's land out from under them."

"Have you mentioned to your daddy how badly
you want the ranch?" he asked.

"Every weekday and twice on Sundays since I hit my teens," she responded with a shrug of resignation. "Daddy doesn't listen to anything that doesn't suit him. You might have noticed that about him."

He had. Trent had a mind of his own and very little interfered with his decisions once they were made. Jake had learned to jump into his boss's thinking process early, when he still had half a chance to sway him. Sara clearly had waited too late, though it seemed likely that Trent had reached this particular decision long before Jake's arrival. Chances were he'd reached it the minute he'd realized he was never going to have a son to whom he could leave his beloved ranch.

Outnumbered by the unexpected number of women in his life, Trent had always viewed Jake as a surrogate son who could help to even the odds in his out-of-balance household.

"Have you told him the lengths to which you're willing to go to keep Three-Stars?" Jake asked.

She shrugged, her expression as resigned as her tone. "It wouldn't make any difference. I figure it's between you and me now."

Jake wasn't willing to let her break her neck *and* lose the ranch. There had to be another way to get her to back off, especially since he had no intention of giving up the land he'd been intent on buying since the day he first set foot on it.

Three-Stars meant more to him than it possibly could to the daughter of Trent Wilde. She'd had a lifetime of privilege. He'd been born to a shiftless father and a drunken mother. Success on the rodeo circuit had given him money and fame, but not the one thing he truly craved…respectability.

"Let's talk about this," he said casually, as if he were giving the idea thoughtful consideration in the face of her determination. "Have you considered the possibility that you could lose?"

Her chin rose a defiant notch. "Not really."

"Well, it is a possibility," he said, figuring if he ought to acknowledge the million-to-one outside chance that she could win, then she'd better at least consider the dead-on certainty that she would lose, not just the bet, but very likely her life. He decided to start small and work up to the big stuff such as breaking her neck.

"It would be pretty humiliating," he pointed out.

"Maybe you're the one who should be worrying about humiliation," she shot right back. "Being beat by a woman would ruin what's left of your reputation with the rodeo set. They'd probably make you give back all those fancy buckles, maybe even take you out of the Pro Rodeo Hall of Fame."

"Not likely." He studied her intently. "So, what's in it for me, if I win?"

She didn't even hesitate. "If you win, and that's a big *if*," she said with cocky confidence, "you get to keep the ranch."

"By tomorrow I'll have a signed contract to buy the ranch," Jake pointed out. "I don't have to climb on another bull and risk breaking a few more of my bones to keep it."

That seemed to throw her. She blinked up at him.

"Isn't owning the ranch free and clear of any claim from me enough?"

"Like I said, it's already mine."

"I could tie it up in court for years, claim you exerted undue influence on my father," she argued.

"Then you'd have to prove he was incompetent to make the decision to sell. Are you prepared to go into court and declare that?"

That silenced her, at least temporarily. Trent might be an ornery old cuss, but no court in Wyoming would find him loony.

Jake doubted Sara was ready to give up, though. As he waited for the other shoe to drop, an outrageous idea popped into his head, one that ought to send her scrambling to put an end to this entire scheme. If he'd been terrified she intended to try to seduce the ranch away from him, how would she feel if he upped the ante to include her? Scared spitless, no doubt.

He regarded her thoughtfully, "Of course, if you cared to up the stakes a little..."

Her gaze narrowed suspiciously. "How?"

He paused as if to ponder the possibilities, then suggested, "First, I'll give you a break. We'll ride broncs, not bulls."

"I don't want any breaks," she insisted.

"Believe me, staying on a bucking bronc for eight seconds will be challenging enough for your spirit of adventure," he said dryly.

Her gaze was fixed on him as if she already guessed there was a catch. He didn't disappoint her.

He smiled. "And if I win, I get the ranch...and you."

She stared at him blankly. "Me?"

"Marriage," he explained patiently.

That ought to scare the bejesus out of her, he thought, even as his own pulse bucked unexpectedly at the prospect. He wasn't the marrying kind, though it struck him that marriage to a woman like Sara Wilde might not be all bad. She'd certainly be full of surprises, no doubt about that.

He called a quick halt to that line of thinking and waited for her to gasp with dismay, blister him for even considering such an insulting proposal, maybe turn tail and flee.

She did none of those things. Instead, after giving the proposal several minutes of thoughtful consideration, she looked him straight in the eye and nodded. "It's a deal," she said quietly.

Then, before he could gather his wits, she turned and walked away, leaving him to wonder just which one of them had gumption and which one was the fool.

Jake was still cursing his impulsiveness when dawn came. Why hadn't he seen that Sara wanted Three-Stars so badly she would have sold her soul to the devil to keep it? He should have recognized that kind of desperation. He'd felt it often enough himself. The truth was, he had seen it. He just hadn't wanted to deal with it. He'd hoped Trent would do it for him. He should have known better. Trent had given up trying to make sense of his daughters long ago. According to local lore, he hadn't had control of any of them since they were toddlers.

So, if he couldn't count on Trent to intervene, Jake figured he would just have to set things right first thing this morning before the whole idiotic plan got out of hand. Nobody was going to be riding broncos. And, sure as hell, nobody was getting married. The very thought made him shudder. His one close brush with the prospect had ended in pure disaster and had nearly cost him his life as well as his career.

Then an image of Sara, silhouetted against his fire the night before, came to mind. He wondered if her skin would be as soft as it appeared, if it would heat at his touch, as his had at hers. He wondered what all that spirit and energy would be like in bed, channeled into wicked, passionate lovemaking.

He cut off that line of thinking before he made himself crazy, so crazy that he would consider going through with the bet just to find out the answers to those questions and all the others that had been plaguing him since he'd found Sara in his house the night before.

Driven by a need to get this resolved, he showered and dressed in record time and headed for the main house, praying he would catch Sara alone. She was often up before her father, as eager to get a start on the day's work as Jake was.

Luck, for once, was on his side. She was seated at the dining room table, an omelet and toast before her, untouched by the look of them. Her appetite was one of the things Jake admired about her. She didn't choose cautiously and pick daintily at her food like most women, who started the day with grapefruit and dry toast. Sara worked hard and ate heartily.

Today, though, it looked as if she might be off her feed. Maybe she was having the same sort of second thoughts about their bargain that he was. It would make things easier.

"Your father around?" Jake asked.

"Actually he went out early this morning," she said, pushing her food around on her plate without tasting it. "He said he had some chores in town."

"Your food's getting cold," Jake commented as he scooped up a healthy serving of scrambled eggs, bacon and toast for himself from the buffet breakfast left by the housekeeper. "Something wrong?"

Cool green eyes rose to clash with his. "What could possibly be wrong?"

"I thought maybe you'd had time to think about what we discussed last night and reached the same conclusion I have."

"And what would that be?"

"That we were both talking a lot of foolishness. You're not going to stay on a bronco for eight seconds and I'm not about to marry you."

She leaned forward. "Are you saying you don't intend to honor our deal?"

"I'm saying we shouldn't go through with it. Let's drop it now, before you get hurt. Last night you were angry. You acted impulsively. I'm sure you regret getting in over your head." Even as the last words spilled from his mouth, Jake realized he'd made a terrible miscalculation. She did not appreciate his attempt at conciliation.

She stood slowly, every magnificent inch of her radiating indignation. "Don't you dare take that condescending tone with me. I knew exactly what I was doing last night," she declared. "The bet is on, Jake Dawson, unless you're too cowardly to go through with it."

The scrambled eggs on his plate were beginning to taste like rubber. Jake slammed down his fork and scowled at her. "Okay, fine. You want to break that pretty little neck of yours, let's do it." He rose and headed for the door.

"Where are you going?"

"To make the arrangements."

Her eyes widened. "Right now?"

"Why wait? There's no time better than the present," he said. "You have a problem with that?"

She shifted uneasily from foot to foot. "Well, actually, I had another date in mind."

"When would that be?"

"A few weeks. A couple of months, maybe."

Jake walked back to her. "What's wrong, sweetheart? Getting cold feet?"

"No," she snapped back at once, but she avoided looking directly at him. "It's just that I'll need a little practice."

The admission came as no surprise to Jake, but it clearly cost her to make it.

"Gee, I thought you were ready to take me on now, get this settled once and for all." He cupped her chin and looked directly into her eyes. "You've broken a horse, haven't you, Sara?"

"Of course. You taught me how."

"Is that what made you think you could win a bet like this?" he asked. "Because if that's it, let me tell you, you don't know the half of it. You're going to spend more time on your butt in the dirt than you ever imagined possible. If you're damned lucky, you won't get trampled in the process."

He forced himself to gentle his angry tone. "There's no shame in taking a good, hard look at reality and deciding maybe this is a bad idea."

"I don't have a choice," she said with an air of weary resignation. "There is no other way. You've made that clear."

Jake almost felt sorry for her, but not sorry enough to tell her father that their deal for the ranch was off. Oh, he could walk away from Sara's challenge, just flat out refuse to play the game she'd devised, but everyone deserved a fighting chance to achieve a dream, didn't they? She needed to know she'd done everything she could if she was going to move on with her life once the ranch was his and his alone.

At least he wouldn't hold her to marriage, when she lost. Suggesting it truly had been a bit of lunacy on his part. Agreeing to it had only shown the depths of her desperation. They were as ill-suited as any two people on the face of the earth could be. There was no point in making two people miserable until the end of time, just because he'd lost his head for a minute.

Now was not the time to get into it, though. Maybe just thinking about being saddled with him for a life-time would keep her on that bronco long enough to make a respectable showing. After all, her pride was at stake here, too, right along with her future.

"See Zeke Laramie," he said grudgingly. "Nobody knows more about rodeo around here than he does."

Her despondent mood instantly lifted. She gave him a saucy grin. "Giving helpful hints to the enemy, Jake? I'm surprised at you."

"I was just thinking maybe he can keep you from getting yourself killed."

What he didn't know was who was going to protect him from getting killed when Trent Wilde found out what his daughter and Jake were up to.

Instead of going to see Zeke Laramie, which was where she intended to go when she left the house, Sara found herself heading into downtown Riverton. A half hour later she was on Dani's doorstep.

Her older sister had a soothing way about her and, Lord knew, Sara needed comfort, maybe a little grounding in reality. Of all the muddles she had gotten herself into in her life, this one had to be the worst.

Not that she could tell Dani about it. She couldn't tell a soul what she had in mind. If her father got wind of the bet she'd made with Jake, he'd probably lock her away in some institution until she was ancient. Unlike any attempt she might make to have her father declared incompetent, his try would be successful. She'd given him all the ammunition he would need to convince any judge in the state that she was mentally off kilter. As far as Jake's proposal, she was still wrestling with that one. He'd probably just hoped to scare her off, which proved he didn't know her at all.

She found her sister in the kitchen as expected, a dusting of flour on the tip of her nose, her dark hair mussed, her hands covered with bread dough as she kneaded it with a vengeance. As Sara watched from the doorway, Dani folded the soft mound in two, then punched it viciously.

"Pretending that's anyone in particular?" Sara inquired with amusement.

Dani glanced up. "Daddy, of course."

The tart response startled her. Sara had long admired Dani's decision to break free from their father's control. She rarely let him ruffle her feathers anymore. Their father must have outdone himself for Dani to be this upset.

"What's he done to you lately?" she asked curiously. She couldn't imagine that he'd told Dani about selling the ranch. Or that Dani would be quite this worked up about it, if he had.

"Oh, he stopped by a little while ago to remind me that I'm not getting any younger," Dani said, slamming a fist into the dough. "As if I couldn't see that for myself. Am I supposed to marry any man who happens along just because Daddy wants to check me off his list of worries?"

Sara grinned. "Is he still trying to pawn Kyle Huggins off on you?"

"I think Daddy sees it as the other way around. After all, Kyle is a catch. He owns his own ranch. He's under eighty. He has no terrible habits to speak of, unless you count chewing tobacco. And he doesn't smell too bad.''

"I wasn't aware you'd been close enough to get a whiff of how he smells," Sara teased. "Is there something you haven't mentioned?"

Dani shot her a baleful look. "One smart-mouthed Wilde in a morning is more than enough."

"You used to admire Kyle," Sara pointed out.

"And I still do. He's an admirable man, but he's old enough to be my father. Heck, maybe even my grandfather. Can you imagine him with a whole passel of little children underfoot?"

"And that's all that matters to you, isn't it? Having kids?"

Dani paused and a familiar dreamy expression spread across her face. Sara had seen that look a million times. Just the sight of a baby was enough to bring it on. Sara only looked like that when she thought about the ranch.

The expression faded, replaced by a deep sadness. "Sometimes my heart aches from wanting to hold my own babies in my arms," Dani admitted in a whisper. She grinned ruefully. "That's not very modern of me, is it?"

"There's nothing wrong with wanting to be a mother," Sara said fiercely. "Maybe you should just go out, find some sexy, suitable stranger and get pregnant."

Dani stared at her. "What an appalling idea!"

"Only because you want the romance and all the trimmings. You wouldn't be the first woman to do something outrageous to get what she wanted in life," Sara said, thinking not so much of Dani now as herself.

Something in her voice must have alerted her big sister that her own mood was just as dark as Dani's. Penetrating brown eyes studied her intently.

"What's up with you?" Dani asked gently. "You didn't ride all the way into town just to listen to me complain about Daddy. Is something up out at the ranch?"

Something was up all right, but she didn't want to be the one to tell Dani about her father's plans. Since she also couldn't explain the restless feelings that had been stirring inside ever since she'd talked to Jake the night before, she forced a carefree smile. "Maybe I just wanted a taste of one of your pies. I bet that's apple I smell in the oven."

"It is and you're not getting any. I have to take an order over to the store by noon. I'm heading over there as soon as I get this bread in the oven."

Sara sighed wistfully. "I remember a time when you baked pies for the family. Now you expect us to go and buy them."

"A woman has to make a living," Dani retorted. "And you can afford my prices."

Sara wandered around the kitchen poking into cupboards, hoping to find a stray chocolate chip cookie at least. "Don't you keep any of the good stuff for yourself?" she asked, when the search came up empty.

"Not so much as a crumb."

"Then I might as well go on home."

"Sara?"

She stopped on her way to the door and faced her sister. Dani's expression was quizzical.

"Are you okay?" she asked. "You don't seem like yourself."

"Exactly who am I?" Sara blurted without thinking. She waved off the question before Dani could even consider a response. "Oh, don't mind me. I guess I just got out of bed on the wrong side this morning."

"Then you're not in need of a deep philosophical discussion on the essence of who we are?"

"I don't think so, but thanks all the same." She came back and hugged her sister, oblivious to the smudges of flour and bits of dough likely to be transferred. "Got to run."

"You heading back to the ranch?"

"Not right away," Sara said, thinking of the visit she intended to pay to Zeke Laramie. "You might say I've got a date with destiny."

Dani clearly didn't take the remark too seriously. She grinned. "Hope he's sexy as hell."

Oddly, it wasn't Zeke's image that came to mind, but Jake's. And, she had to admit, he was sexy as hell. Last night, when he'd suggested making marriage part of the bet, she hadn't been nearly as appalled or outraged as she should have been. Instead, her fool heart had reacted as if the idea were something other than totally preposterous.

It was absurd, of course. The man was out to steal the only thing that mattered to her. That made him the enemy, a scoundrel, a devious snake in the grass.

She would not, under any circumstances, marry such a man, sexy or not. Which made getting over to see Zeke Laramie more critical than ever.

Chapter Three

Zeke Laramie was as bent and scarred as a centuries-old weathered tree. He walked with an uneven, painful gait that had Sara wincing as she watched him. She knew for a fact that old injuries had pretty much torn up one knee, both hips and a shoulder.

Local legends had grown up around Zeke's once glorious rodeo career and the spectacular, bone-breaking tumbles he occasionally took. She hadn't needed Jake to tell her that Zeke was one of the best. She'd hardly dared to think that he might be willing to teach her what he knew, but with Jake's recommendation maybe he would.

Unfortunately when Zeke spotted her crossing the lawn toward the paddock where he was working, his leathery face creased with a suspicious frown. Zeke was also notorious for his lack of welcome.

His circle of friends was limited. Beyond Jake, Sara couldn't think of a single person who claimed to be intimately acquainted with him. She had never met him before, nor even seen him in town. Visitors came to his small horse ranch at their own peril. They were as likely to be greeted with a shotgun as a smile, depending on his mood.

"What do you want?" he demanded ungraciously. "If you're trying to sell me something, you can turn right on around and git."

"I'm Sara Wilde," she said, holding out her hand. Zeke ignored it. "So?"

"I thought maybe Jake Dawson might have called you about me."

At the mention of Jake's name, his expression softened almost imperceptibly. He looked her up and down. Sara got the distinct impression that she didn't measure up. The hard glint returned at once to his eyes.

"You know Jake?" he asked, as if he couldn't quite believe it.

"He works for my father, Trent Wilde."

Zeke nodded, no more impressed by that than he had been by the mention of Jake. Perhaps he was the only man in the entire state of Wyoming not awed by Trent Wilde. Sara decided she could forgive him a lot of rudeness just for that.

"Actually, Jake is the reason I'm here. I need a little help with something and he recommended you."

"Ain't taking on any new horses right now," Zeke said. "I've got my hands full as it is."

"It's not about a horse," she said, then amended, "exactly."

Zeke regarded her impatiently. "Which is it?"

"I need you to teach me to stay on a bronco."

The old man's mouth gaped comically. Then he started to chuckle. The chuckle blossomed into a gut-deep laugh. He laughed so hard his eyes watered. He whipped off his hat and slapped his knee with it.

Sara was delighted he was having so much enjoyment at her expense. Maybe since she had brightened his day so, he would look on her request more favorably.

"I'm serious," she insisted, when he'd calmed down.

"And I'm the bloody Queen of England." He shook his head. "You on a bronc. If that don't beat all. Jake put you up to this, didn't he? Wanted to give me the best laugh I've had in a month of Sundays, I'll bet. You go on back and tell him it worked."

He settled his hat back on his head and turned away, chuckling once more as he headed back into the paddock.

"Mr. Laramie?"

He kept right on walking. He didn't even glance back. "Go on. You can git now," he said. "You've had your fun."

"Mr. Laramie!" Sara repeated more emphatically. "I'll pay you a thousand dollars for the lessons."

That snagged his attention. Money usually talked, sometimes even more effectively than reason, she'd found to her disappointment.

He turned slowly and stared at her. "I'm too old to be foolin' with this kinda nonsense. You want lessons, get Jake to teach you. I taught him everything he knows."

Sara shook her head. "That won't work."

"Why the hell not? He's right there under your nose."

"True, but my bet's with him."

Zeke's eyes nearly popped out of his head. "You made some kinda fool bet with Jake?"

He sounded vaguely intrigued by that, so Sara decided to take full advantage of his fascination. She winked.

"Just between you and me?" she asked in a conspiratorial whisper.

"You see anybody else around?" he grumbled.

"Okay, here's the deal," she said, confident his attention was riveted on her. "I suppose you could say I bet the farm on my beating Jake in a bronc riding contest."

Zeke just stared. "You're serious? You bet Three-Stars?"

"Every acre of it."

"Well, I'll be damned," he said, clearly awestruck. "And Jake agreed to this?"

She grinned. "He took a little persuading, since he already considers the ranch to be all but his."

"His? How'd that come about?"

Sara gestured dismissively. "Oh, he made some sort of arrangement with my father. I stepped in before they signed and made Jake an offer of my own."

"Must have been quite an offer."

"One he couldn't resist," she said cheerfully. "That's when he sent me to you. He figured you were the only one around who could keep me from getting killed. His words, by the way."

"Probably am," Zeke agreed. "How much time do I have?"

"A few weeks," Sara said, sensing victory in this battle at least. "Will you do it?"

"I will," he said solemnly. "And you can keep your thousand bucks. I'll do it just to see the look on Jake's face when you win."

Impulsively, Sara threw her arms around him. "You think I can do it? You think I can win?"

Zeke blushed fiery red with embarrassment and hurriedly stepped out of her embrace. "Would I be risking my reputation, if I didn't?" He regarded her slyly. "Besides, it's about time some woman came along and stirred that boy into a tizzy. He's been alone too danged long. Something tells me you've got just the right mix of gumption and daring to be a good match for him."

The comment alerted Sara that Zeke just might be misinterpreting the nature of her bet. "This isn't personal between Jake and me," she insisted.

"Girl, a bet is always personal, especially when a man's pride or his land is at stake."

Sara suddenly swallowed hard. Even though she'd thrown the possibility of humiliation right back into Jake's face the night before, she hadn't really considered what it would mean for him to lose. Jake was going to be fighting for more than Three-Stars. He was going to be battling to hang on to his reputation.

Forget his experience, which already gave him an edge, a man with so much at risk might very well be impossible to beat, especially by an amateur.

Sara might have been daunted by the seemingly insurmountable odds of winning, if it hadn't been for Zeke's blustery confidence in his own skill as an instructor. She had sheer desperation working in her favor as well. She couldn't afford to let anything like cool reason shake her confidence.

Zeke surveyed her worriedly. "You ain't scared, are you?"

"Of what?" she retorted blithely. "Losing?"

"No, indeed, I was talking about getting thrown. If you're scared of that, we might as well quit before we start."

"Mr. Laramie, I'm not afraid of anything except losing my home." And maybe of the feelings Jake stirred in her, but that was another thing altogether.

"That's good. You be here at eight a.m. sharp tomorrow," Zeke told her. "There was a lot of men happy to see Jake busted up and out of rodeo, so's they could have a shot at the top spot. He ain't going to be no pushover, just because you're a woman. I'd say we have our work cut out for us."

Sara nodded, fighting a queasy sensation in the pit of her stomach. Oh, yeah. Let the games begin.

"Did she call you?" Jake asked Zeke when he phoned him after supper that night.

It was the second time they'd spoken that day. That was more than they'd talked in the last month. Zeke wasn't big on phones. He claimed the infernal contraptions interfered with his love life. Since he'd been married to the same woman for close to fifty years, it raised some interesting theories on what kept their marriage intact. In fact, Zeke's relationship with his beloved Mary Lou was about the only example Jake could recall of a marriage he could honestly admire. Given Zeke's crusty temperament, he considered their staying power a miracle and Mary Lou a saint.

"I assume you're referring to my new client," Zeke said, his tone huffy. "She didn't call. She came by. Pretty little thing. You didn't mention that when you told me to expect to hear from her."

"I hadn't noticed," Jake lied.

"Then your eyesight must be failing," Zeke retorted.

Jake ignored the remark. "You didn't tell her we'd talked, did you?"

"Dang boy, I told you I wouldn't. You know I keep my word."

"I know. I'm sorry," Jake apologized. "It's just that this whole fool thing has me tied up in knots."

"I can imagine. You didn't tell me about the bet. What possessed you to get involved in anything so crazy?"

"Did she happen to mention what's at stake?"

"You mean aside from your pride and her neck? Yeah, she did say something about the ranch, too. Frankly, that's what has me buffaloed. Since I first ran across you, all you talked about was getting your hands on some land of your own. Now you've got your chance and you're risking it. How come?"

"Because running Three-Stars was her dream, too. It's not her fault that her father's a chauvinistic old fool. Besides, I figure it's a safe bet."

"You're forgetting who's teaching her," Zeke reminded him. "You sent her to the best."

"Face it, old man, not even you are up to this challenge."

"Oh, I don't know. She looks like a winner to me. Anyone with as much heart as she has shows potential."

"Dammit, Zeke, if anything happens to her, I'm holding you accountable."

"I'm not the one who made an idiotic bet with her in the first place," Zeke reminded him.

Jake sighed. "No, I did that all on my own."

"Must have been blinded by love," Zeke guessed, sounding a little too gleeful. "Ever since I told Mary Lou about all this, she's been all atwitter thinking about a wedding for the two of you."

Given Mary Lou's love of matchmaking, Jake was relieved he hadn't mentioned his impulsive inclusion of a marriage rider to the contest rules. "Don't start with me, old man. Just keep Sara in one piece, okay?" He paused, then added, "And keep Mary Lou the hell away from her."

Zeke chuckled at that. "Must mean the thought's crossed your mind, if you're all nervous about it."

Jake refused to rise to the bait. "You know my opinion of marriage, Zeke. If my parents hadn't taught me that, that brush with Sue Ann would have soured me for good. It's strictly a fool's game. You and Mary Lou excepted, of course."

"It's a dull man whose mind can't be opened to new ideas."

"If you want to preach, go find a church. I'm way too old to listen to your dime store philosophy."

"And I'm too old to be caught up in your shenanigans. How about I call Miss Sara Wilde and tell her the deal's off?"

Jake was all for that. But he knew it wouldn't be the end of it. Sara would just go and find someone else to teach her and that someone else wasn't likely to know half of what Zeke Laramie knew.

"No," Jake said emphatically. "I want you to work with her, no one else."

"Then that's the way it'll be," Zeke said readily. He allowed the subject to rest for a beat, then added, "Still say you're sweet on her, though."

Zeke hung up before Jake could argue with him. He might find Sara Wilde attractive. He might even find her intriguing. But there wasn't a woman alive who would ever tempt him to walk down the aisle of a church and say a bunch of vows that didn't amount to a hill of beans.

It suddenly struck him, though, that there was a whole lot of fascinating territory that could be explored before a man ever had to say I do.

Anticipating her first bronc-riding lesson, Sara could barely choke down a piece of toast at breakfast the next morning. Worse, she was sitting at the table under her father's watchful, perplexed gaze. She would have bolted from the dining room, but that would only have alarmed him and brought him chasing after her.

He'd always been the nosiest, most protective son of a gun on the face of the earth. The trait had only gotten worse since Dani and Ashley had left home. Most days that left Sara virtually alone as the focus for his attention and his worrying. Yesterday's visit to aggravate Dani had been a rare exception. Obviously he was hoping to get at least one of them settled before he took off on this secret fling of his.

"You're not eating much this morning, Sara Jane," her father noted. "Everything okay?"

Since she couldn't tell him that she was going to extraordinary means to resurrect the future he'd just single-handedly destroyed, she forced a smile.

"Terrific," she said tightly and rushed to change the subject. "By the way, I understand you paid a visit to Dani yesterday. When are you going to give up on the idea of marrying her off to Kyle Huggins?"

"When she's married to somebody else," he said unrepentantly.

"A woman doesn't have to be married to be happy," Sara pointed out.

"Your sister does. She wants babies. Only one way I know to get them."

"I suggested she just find a handsome stranger and get pregnant," Sara countered cheerfully.

Bright patches of red flamed in her father's cheeks. "Sara Jane, I will not have that kind of talk in my house. I raised you and your sisters to know right from wrong."

"You also raised us to go after what we wanted."

He frowned. "Within the bounds of good taste."

"Who set the rules?" she asked. "You?"

"Me, Emily Post, Miss Manners, what does it matter? Right's right," he said stubbornly.

"Tell me, Daddy, if you'd seen some way to have a son without Mama being the wiser about your indiscretion, would you have gone for it? Did you ever consider just adopting a little boy, when the two of you kept producing girls?"

His frown deepened. "What the devil brought on a bunch of fool questions like that?"

Sara swallowed all of the pent up resentment that had been guiding her actions the past couple of days. Arguing wouldn't accomplish a thing anyway. She slid her chair back from the table.

"Never mind. I've got to be going. I have an appointment."

Her father seemed as eager as she was to let the subject of sons and babies rest. "Getting your hair done?" he asked.

The question was so typical of her father's thought processes that Sara cringed. Naturally he didn't anticipate that she might have an actual business appointment or even chores around the ranch.

"No," she said, then added truthfully, albeit with an edge of sarcasm, "I'm going to take a bronc-riding lesson."

He laughed heartily at that. "Okay, so don't tell me what you're up to. I suppose you're entitled to your secrets, same as the rest of us."

"That's right, Daddy, and you're just full of them, aren't you?"

She walked away, ignoring his shouted demand to know what she meant by that. Fuming, she slammed open the kitchen door and ran smack into a grinning Jake.

"Careful, sweetheart."

"Oh, just stay out of my way," she snapped.

"Actually, I was referring to your tendency to mouth off without thinking. Unless, of course, you're hoping your father will figure out that you really are preparing to ride a bronco and that he'll put a stop to it. That would save your pretty little tush, wouldn't it?"

"You were eavesdropping," she accused.

"The cows in the west forty probably heard your conversation. Neither one of you has a volume control when you're arguing." He grinned. "Did you really tell your sister to just go out and get pregnant?"

"I did." She regarded him speculatively. "Are you interested in volunteering?"

"Not likely." A dangerous gleam flickered in his eyes. "I've got my hands full with you."

"What you and I have going boils down to an eight-second contest," she countered. "That should leave you plenty of time for chasing any other women who interest you."

He shook his head. "I don't think so."

That glint in his eyes intensified, startling her. An intensity that hot could have singed brick. Sara swallowed hard. "Eight seconds," she repeated adamantly.

"Not nearly long enough for what I have in mind," he said in a low, provocative voice.

Sara stared. What the devil was he up to?

He reached out and deliberately trailed a callused finger along the curve of her lips. A shiver of pure delight shimmied down her spine. She reached up to remove his hand, but he caught her hand in midair and brought it to his mouth. The kiss he grazed across her knuckles was soft and warm and sweet. Sara simply stared at him, bemused by the unexpected tenderness.

Trying to gather her wits, she backed away a step and found herself pinned against the counter. Jake followed, bracing an arm on either side of her, his thighs and hips so close she could feel his heat. The warm, male scent of him surrounded her.

"This isn't part of our deal," she whispered, her voice choked.

"Sure, it is," he claimed. "If I'm going to marry a woman, I surely should know what I'm getting, don't you think?"

"This isn't some ice-cream store, where they'll give you a spoonful before you commit to a pint," she retorted, trying to wriggle away from him. Her frantic movements only seemed to amuse him.

Then the sparks of laughter in his eyes suddenly turned serious as he bent forward very, very slowly and touched his mouth to hers.

Sara could have sworn lightning split the sky and thunder boomed at precisely that moment. Certainly fireworks went off. The reaction was devastating, setting off ten years of pent up lust. It took every ounce of willpower she possessed to keep from flinging her arms around his neck and her legs around his waist and taking him right there on the kitchen floor. This reaction wouldn't do. He might get the idea she was actually eager to marry him when nothing could be further from the truth.

His kiss was more controlled, more deliberate than she wanted. He coaxed and persuaded and taunted. She was weak-kneed and trembling before his tongue ever skimmed her own. That set off another round of lightning, thunder and fireworks, plus what sounded like a crash of cymbals.

Awestruck by the effect and desperate for more, she fought disappointment when he pulled away.

"Jake?" she implored, gazing into eyes every bit as dazed as her own.

"I think we're in Annie's way," he murmured.

For a moment, Sara couldn't think who the heck Annie was or why she had anything to do with ending such a glorious, monumental kiss. Then she connected Annie and the cymbals. Apparently the housekeeper had been slamming around a few pots and pans to get their attention.

"Oh, geez," she murmured, as heat flooded into her cheeks. Annie was the next best thing she had to a mother and she had just caught Sara and Jake making out in her kitchen.

Apparently guessing her embarrassment from her expression, Jake offered a reassuring smile. "Don't worry. She won't talk. Annie and I have a deal. She never discusses what she catches me doing in her kitchen, isn't that right, Annie?''

Sara was intrigued despite herself. ''Exactly what kinds of things has she caught you doing?''

''I'll never tell,'' Annie said dutifully, winking at Jake.

''And neither will I,'' Jake said. ''By the way, didn't you say something to your father about an appointment?''

Sara glanced at the clock. It was almost eight. She was going to be late to her first appointment with Zeke. Something told her he wasn't going to be happy about it. Jake admitted that he heard her tell her dad about the bronc riding lessons, so of course he knew where she was going.

She regarded Jake suspiciously. ''You did that on purpose, didn't you?''

He returned her look innocently. ''Did what?''

''Tried to make me late.''

''Not me,'' he swore. ''I just developed this sudden urge for a little sugar before breakfast.''

Annie guffawed at that. For a woman who'd practically raised all three of the Wilde sisters, her loyalties seemed somewhat misdirected. No doubt Jake had that effect on a lot of women. Sara scowled at the pair of them.

''Well, next time you're in the kitchen and decide you want a little sugar,'' Sara said, ''I suggest you try the pantry. Just make sure you avoid the kind that's laced with arsenic for the other rats.''

Chapter Four

Admiring her spirit, if not her assessment of his moral character, Jake watched with masculine appreciation as Sara sashayed out of the kitchen. Deliberate or not, the taunting swing of her hips in those formfitting denims was enough to make a man's blood sizzle. Combined with that seemingly unconscious seductiveness she'd displayed at his house, it added up to one dangerously provocative woman.

"You hurt that girl and you'll answer to me," Annie O'Leary announced, waving a rolling pin at him menacingly. "And that's before Mr. Wilde gets his hands on you."

Somewhat daunted by the unexpectedly serious warning, Jake deliberately tried to lighten the mood by dropping a kiss on the housekeeper's furrowed forehead, bringing a blush to her round cheeks. "I thought you adored me, Annie, my love."

"How I feel about you isn't the issue. It's how I feel about that girl. I love her as much as if she were my own and I won't see her hurt."

She said it as if Sara were some fragile little thing, incapable of looking after herself. Jake knew otherwise. "Trust me, Annie, Sara's no shrinking violet. She can take care of herself."

Annie wasn't persuaded. "I don't doubt it in most situations, but she hasn't met up with the likes of you all that often. You're handsome as sin and twice as dangerous. More experienced women than Sara have been taken in by that crooked smile of yours. I daresay more than one has come to the conclusion that marriage is in the cards, only to discover they were playing with the wrong deck."

Jake flinched at the direct hit. "I can't help it if some woman gets foolish ideas about the future. My opinion of marriage is no secret. I lay it out at the beginning. Anything that comes after is done at their own, fully informed risk."

"Hogwash! A woman who's interested in a man will say whatever she figures he wants to hear at the beginning," Annie insisted. "Like it or not, that so-called first-date disclaimer of yours doesn't absolve you of any responsibility for any hurt that comes after."

"That's not my problem," he repeated defensively. "Fifteen years of watching my mother and father try to destroy each other under the guise of commitment was more than enough. I'll take bachelorhood over that any day and anyone who knows me at all is aware of that.''

Annie's expression turned momentarily sympathetic. ''From everything you've said and a lot more you haven't, I know it wasn't easy for you growing up around those two, but you shouldn't let it shape your whole life.''

''Whose genes are running through my blood?'' he countered. ''I've got a double dose of the worst temperaments this side of hell. I'm not going to inflict myself on some unsuspecting woman so that we can both be miserable.''

''You might be surprised how your view of life changes with the right woman around,'' Annie said. Her expression softened. ''Sue Ann wasn't that woman.''

''And you just told me to stay away from Sara.''

''She's not the right woman, either,'' Annie said fiercely. ''But there's one out there for you. I guarantee it. You just have to open your heart and let her in, once she shows up.''

''You're nothing but a soft-hearted romantic,'' Jake accused affectionately. ''Next thing you'll be saying there's a woman out there who could put up with Trent Wilde, now that he's been spoiled all these years by you and his wife.''

''There probably is,'' she countered complacently. ''Not that he's looking for a replacement for his wife. He's just looking to kick up his heels a bit, to start living again. It's been lonely for him these past two years.''

Jake regarded her intently. "You know about his plans, don't you?"

Annie promptly looked guilty. "I wasn't supposed to say anything, but I figured that didn't include you, since you're mixed up in this. If you ask me, he's acting like an old fool, no disrespect intended."

Jake opened his mouth to protest, but Annie waved him off.

"Not that I don't want you to have this place," she said. "I know how hard you've worked for it and how badly you want to own it. But Mr. Wilde is going off without a thought in his head about what's to come of his girls. He's shirking his responsibilities, if you ask me."

"Her father's trying to get Dani settled down before he goes. Ashley's already successful doing exactly what she always wanted."

"And what about Sara?" Annie demanded. "What does he have planned for her? This ranch is the only thing that girl has ever cared two hoots about. Is she supposed to trail along with him to Arizona? Or maybe go work for some other rancher? He's just assuming she'll marry one day, but what if she doesn't?"

"She'll always have a place here," Jake said impulsively.

Annie's eyebrows rose. "Meaning?"

"Meaning that she knows this ranch inside out. If she wants to stick around, she can work for me."

Annie hooted at that. "You expect her to hire on as a hand on the ranch that should have been left to her? Her pride will never let her do that and you know it.''

Jake shrugged. ''I'm just saying the option's there if she wants it.''

''Well, if that was supposed to reassure me, it doesn't. I suppose I'm the one who's going to have to sit Mr. Wilde down and explain his responsibilities to him.''

''Invite me along,'' Jake suggested. ''I'd like to hear that. It should be better entertainment than what the Old West Grill puts on on Saturday night.''

The sudden bellowing of his name prevented Jake from going on.

''Dammit, boy, stop hanging out in the kitchen and get in here,'' Trent shouted. ''We've got to look over these papers the attorney left yesterday. I thought you were anxious to get things settled.''

Jake glanced back at Annie, whose expression had turned resigned. ''It's too late, Annie, my love. This horse is out of the barn.''

Her chin thrust out stubbornly. ''You're discounting my powers of persuasion and the love that man has for his daughters. Once he sees what he's doing to Sara, he'll change his mind.''

Something ran cold deep inside Jake at the conviction in her voice. ''Never,'' he said, equally adamant.

He walked out of the kitchen before Annie could say anything that might convince him that she had the power to do what none of the rest of them could...change Trent Wilde's mind.

* * *

Sara's butt felt as if she'd been paddled with a two-by-four. The expression "eat dirt" had taken on new meaning. In fact, she'd hit the ground so hard her teeth had rattled.

The horse responsible was now munching on hay as calmly as if he'd spent the morning loafing in his stall. He hadn't even worked up a good lather.

She eyed the big roan balefully. She had a feeling she could grow to despise the beautiful creature before this was over. And he was the most docile in Zeke's barn or so he claimed. She'd barely settled in the saddle before he'd launched her in the air with no more than a violent kick of those powerful back legs.

"That's it for the day," Zeke said, offering a hand to drag her to her feet.

Sara ignored it and leapt up. "Come on, Zeke. One more time."

"Girl, you got more grit than sense," Zeke told her, shaking his head.

"Somehow that sounds like a compliment, when you say it," Sara retorted. "Please, one more time."

"Nope. You'll be sore enough as it is. Git on home and soak in a hot tub filled with some Epsom Salts. You'll thank me in the morning."

Since it seemed unlikely she was going to change his mind, Sara gave up. How had she managed to surround herself with such stubborn males? Was she ever likely to be able to do things her own way again?

That's what the bet was all about, she reminded

herself sternly. Once she beat Jake and owned Three-Stars outright, she would never have to answer to anyone again.

Keeping that goal in mind was all that had gotten her through this first painful, humiliating lesson. She might have been thoroughly discouraged by her inability to remain on the horse for more than a nano-second, if Zeke hadn't been so lavish with his praise. He was a great instructor—tough, but quick to point out the minute successes, rather than the obvious failures.

"Was Jake this bad when he started?" she asked, despite her determination not to pry for information about the man who'd practically kissed her senseless a few hours earlier.

Zeke hesitated, avoiding her gaze. When he finally looked at her, he said, "I won't lie to you. Jake was a natural. But being a winner is as much about character as it is about inborn skill. I can teach you the skills, but if you don't have the will to stick with it, nothing I show you is going to help."

"I'm not giving up," Sara said grimly.

Zeke nodded approvingly. "Never thought you would. See you again first thing tomorrow, though I'm predicting that a few hours from now you're going to hate me for putting your body through this torture. You'll be ready to go check yourself into some fancy spa where they can pamper you."

"Never," she promised. A few aches and pains were a small price to pay for Three-Stars.

By the time she got back to the ranch, though, she was beginning to have little twinges in every muscle she possessed. She didn't hate Zeke at that moment, but she was beginning to reassess her opinion of him. It was entirely possible that he was some sort of evil sadist, who thrived on inflicting pain.

She was limping toward the house, when she spotted Jake. Before she could make an agonizing dash from view, he caught sight of her. She forced herself to straighten up and walk as if she were in perfect health.

"How'd the first lesson go?" he asked.

Sara plastered on her very brightest smile. She knew the value of psychological warfare as well as anyone. "Terrific. Zeke says this is going to be a breeze. He claims I'm a natural, practically as good as you were when you started."

The stark lie didn't appear to fool Jake.

"Oh, really?" he said skeptically. He reached for her left hand and examined it with painstaking intensity. "No bruises. No raw spots. That must mean the reins didn't stay wrapped around your hand for long." He lifted his gaze to meet hers. "Take any spills?"

"Not a one," she lied.

"Then I guess you must have been rolling around in the dirt just for fun." He reached over and brushed a streak of dust from her shoulder. He was aiming for another one on the seat of her jeans, when she backed out of reach.

"The horse must have been kicking up more dirt than I realized," she said. "Excuse me, but I'm going in to check my messages and clean up a little."

His eyes sparked with mischief. "Now why do I find that image so fascinating?"

"Because you're depraved," she suggested sweetly and stalked away.

Jake's voice followed her. "If you expect to move later, a long hot bath would be in order."

"I'll keep that in mind."

"I could come inside and run it for you."

"In your dreams. Besides, I have chores to do. I'll shower later."

An hour later, after running a brush through her hair and washing the dirt off her face, Sara could already feel her muscles stiffening. She eyed her tub longingly, but reminded herself she didn't dare let Jake see any hint of weakness. If she didn't show up to clean out the stalls and feed the horses this afternoon, he would know that the lesson had gotten to her. She dragged herself out to the barn, wincing with every step.

The instant she saw him, though, she forced herself to move with a normal stride.

Jake leaned back against the gate to an unoccupied stall and surveyed her from head to toe. "You cleaned up pretty good. How're you feeling?"

"I told you before, I'm just fine," she snapped, reaching for a broom. The effort very nearly brought tears to her eyes. Aside from the bumps and bruises she'd discovered when she'd peeked under her clothes, her arms and shoulders felt as if she'd tried to tug a speeding train to a halt.

Jake just stood where he was and observed every move she made. It forced her to keep up the pretense long past the time when any sane person would have given up and begged for some soothing liniment and a massage.

"Give me that," Jake finally said irritably. He snatched the broom from her. "Go on inside and rest."

Sara tried to drag it back, but her muscles protested vehemently. She was forced to relinquish the broom, along with the first little sliver of her pride. She wondered how much more Jake would claim before they were done.

"You could do me a favor," he said as he swept.

"What?"

"If you're not too beat, take a look at the books for me. There's a mistake in there somewhere, but I'll be damned if I can find it."

Suspicious, Sara regarded him intently. "Is there really a mistake or is this just your way of giving me desk duty for the afternoon?"

"Trust me, there's a mistake. I figure fresh eyes might be able to find it. You're better with numbers than I am anyway."

For some reason the scant praise pleased her far more than it should have. It also made her wonder a little wistfully if she and Jake might not have made good partners, if things had been different.

She glanced up and realized that Jake had stopped sweeping. His gaze was fixed on her. The intense expression in his eyes was enough to set off that unfamiliar trembling in the pit of her stomach all over again.

"I'll get right on it," she promised, heading for the house.

"If you find it, dinner's on me," he called after her.

Stunned by the apparent invitation, Sara turned back to stare. "Are you asking me out?"

He shrugged, but his bold gaze remained riveted on her. "I'm offering you a bribe for doing the books," he corrected.

Sara nodded. "As long as we're clear about it."

"I always try to make my intentions crystal clear, sweetheart."

Sara's breath snagged in her throat. She wondered if he knew that the look in his eyes indicated far different intentions than his words had.

Jake wasn't sure what had possessed him to ask Sara to dinner. Maybe it was a perverse reaction to Annie's warning to steer clear of her. Maybe it was admiration for the way she'd tackled her chores even though she was visibly sore and exhausted.

Or maybe it was simply the fact that now that he'd noticed her as a woman, his hormones had kicked in with predictable results. On a purely physical level he wanted her and dinner was a prelude to getting what he wanted. Flirting and seduction were second nature to him. He could no more have ignored that pull than his horse could resist nosing his pockets in search of sugar.

He had no doubt that dinner was a done deal, either. There had been no false flattery in his claim that Sara was a whiz with the books. He lost patience when the mistakes weren't obvious, but she was content to fiddle with the numbers like a skein of twisted yarn until she found the right thread to untangle the puzzle.

Showered and changed, Jake went up to the main house. He used the separate entrance to the office Trent had created specifically for him and decorated with family cast-off furniture. It was next to his own. Sara was in there as often as Jake was, though it was doubtful her father knew that.

Jake loved this room even more than his boss's larger office. Panelled in rich, dark wood, one wall was filled with bookcases, another with a huge painting of a rodeo rider that managed to capture every bit of the agony and joy of the sport. That painting reminded Jake of the difficult path he'd chosen and the rewards that were finally within reach.

The scarred desk and ancient leather chair had the look of well-used heirlooms, something that had been in short supply in Jake's life. When Trent had offered to replace both with something newer and fancier, Jake had declined.

He loved rubbing his fingers over the nicks and scratches in the desk and thinking of the men who'd used it before him. When he sank into the chair, he couldn't help thinking of its history and wondering if Trent Wilde's ancestors would have been proud to claim a man like him, as his own father wasn't.

Frank Dawson had never even bothered to come to the rodeo to see him ride. And if he had, Jake conceded ruefully, he probably would have been blind drunk anyway.

This room, which had once been used for little more than storage for the bigger office beyond, suited him. Amidst its very masculine, solid decor, he could make believe that he was a man of substance, a man without pretense, when the exact opposite was true. Here he could achieve some vague sense of what it might have been like to have a proud history. Trent might dismiss the furnishings as little more than old junk, but Jake thought otherwise.

The only modern concession in the room was the computer. That was where he expected to find Sara, her brow furrowed in concentration, the tip of her tongue caught between her teeth as she studied the screen.

Instead, she was curled up in the matching leather chair by the fire, her eyes closed. The image brought a smile to his lips. Finding Sara snuggled into one of his chairs was getting to be a habit, one he could get used to, he feared.

Drawn despite himself, he crossed the room silently and stood over her. She'd showered and changed since he'd seen her. Her cheek was flushed where it rested against her arms. Her hair, that glorious tangle of fire, was dangerously beguiling. Her lashes feathered against her cheeks in dark smudges that seemed tipped in gold.

Something hard and cold inside him melted at the sight. The sensation shook him as nothing else in his life ever had. This thing with Sara was a familiar game, nothing more, he vowed silently.

To prove it, he moved to his desk and focused on

the computer screen, pretending she wasn't even in the room.

Within minutes, he knew it was no use. He was aware of her with every fiber of his being. Much later, he knew the precise instant when she stirred.

Glancing sideways he saw her eyelids flutter, then open. A vision of her in bed, coming sleepily, sexily awake in his arms ripped through him. It was so vivid, so real that his blood heated and surged through him, leaving him aching in a way that would, no doubt, keep him awake half the night.

He shifted uncomfortably and drew her startled gaze.

"Oh, my," she murmured sleepily. "I must have fallen asleep. When did you get here?"

"A couple of hours ago," Jake said, concentrating very hard on calming his rampaging hormones.

"And you just let me sleep?"

"It seemed like the gentlemanly thing to do."

Her lips curved. "I'm disappointed, Jake. I was so certain you were no gentleman."

The taunting remark stirred his passion and his temper in equal measure. "You're doing it again," he said, gritting his teeth.

"Doing what?"

"Trying to provoke me."

She blinked, her expression so innocent he could almost believe it wasn't an act.

"How?" she asked.

"By throwing all those innuendoes and subtle dares in my face. I'm warning you, you're flirting with disaster, sweetheart."

Her grin then was slow and deliberate and very definitely provocative. "Oh, dear, and here I thought I was flirting with you."

The taunt made Jake's head spin. He was on his feet in a heartbeat, across the room in two.

And then Sara was in his arms, her body crushed against his as his mouth plundered hers. She might have been exhausted. Hell, she might have been half asleep, but she came fully awake at once.

Jake's intentions might have been to shock and take, but he was the one who wound up surprised. Sara gave everything to that kiss, willingly, eagerly.

They were both breathing hard when Jake finally pulled away and shook his head to clear it. He gazed into green eyes that sparked with passion and questions.

Questions he couldn't—or wouldn't—answer.

"It would be a disaster," he muttered, half to himself.

"What would be?"

"You and me."

To his amazement once more, she smiled knowingly. "You were the one who made marriage part of the deal, Jake. Isn't it nice to know that we won't be bored in bed?"

Before he could form a coherent response to that, she was gone. And he was left to another restless, lonely night.

Chapter Five

Kissing Sara Wilde could get to be habit-forming, Jake concluded during a long and very restless night. He was relieved that he'd be heading out first thing this morning for a two-day check of the fence lines. Time and distance would surely cure him of this unwanted fascination with the boss's daughter. Women rarely tangled up his emotions for more than forty-eight hours at a stretch, especially when he gave his common sense time to kick into gear.

Just to be sure there would be no last-minute temptations, he avoided the dining room, grabbed a bowl of oatmeal in the kitchen and settled down to eat it under Annie's watchful eye. That was almost more disconcerting than dealing with Sara.

"You seem to be in some sort of hurry this morning," Annie observed.

"I've got miles of fence to check. It's going to be a long day."

The corners of the woman's mouth twitched with some private amusement. "Must be quite a project. You're the second person to tell me that this morning."

Jake paused, a spoonful of oatmeal halfway to his mouth. "And the other one was...?" he asked unnecessarily. Trent Wilde hadn't mended a fence line himself in years.

"Sara," Annie said, confirming his worst fears. "She was up with the chickens. Bolted her food down, too."

Jake carefully set the spoon back down and eyed the housekeeper warily. "Sara said something about checking fences?"

"Sure did. She said you wanted to get an early start. She's already out in the barn saddling up. I sent the packs of food along with her."

"What the devil...?" Jake pushed away from the table, grabbed his Stetson and headed for the door.

"Jake Dawson, you can't work all morning on half a bowl of cereal," Annie called after him.

"I'll eat Sara's share of the food you packed for a midmorning snack," he retorted. There was no way in hell she was going to need it.

Sure enough, though, Sara was in the barn. She greeted him with a cheerful smile that almost melted his grim determination to set her straight about going along on this two-day trip with him.

"What are you up to?" he inquired.

"What does it look like?" she asked as she

cinched the saddle securely. "We have a fence line to check. I saw the note on your calendar. You must have forgotten to mention it last night."

"*I* have a fence line to check," he corrected.

"We've been through this before. It's my ranch. I should see firsthand what repairs are needed."

"It is not your ranch," Jake retorted grimly. "Besides, I thought you had a lesson with Zeke today."

"I called and postponed it until tomorrow evening."

"I'll bet he loved that."

Sara shrugged. "He understood that chores come first on a ranch. If I neglect the fences, we could lose cattle."

Jake clung to his patience by a thread. "The fence won't be neglected. I'll be checking it."

"We'll get done that much faster if we both do it," she said cheerfully. "I'm ready whenever you are."

Jake muttered a curse under his breath and stalked to the stall where his own horse was waiting impatiently. He couldn't order Sara not to come. In truth, it wouldn't be the first time they had shared a chore like this.

But it would be the first time since he'd discovered that she was capable of tormenting his senses. He suspected that she was well aware of the impact she had on him and had deliberately forced the issue just to make him crazy. He doubted she had any idea, though, just how dangerous a game she was playing. Last time he'd checked, he'd been a long way off from sainthood. The kisses they'd shared should have told her that, too.

"Suit yourself," he said finally.

"I always do."

"I'm just surprised that you're taking time off from training already," he said slyly. "Was the first day too much for you, after all?"

Sara scowled at him. "I explained that chores come first."

"I know that's what you said," he agreed.

"Meaning?"

"That it looks an awful lot to me as if you're chickening out on our bet. Looks to me like you latched on to the first excuse that came along to avoid getting back on that bronco. Which one did Zeke put you on? Lightning or Jezebel?"

"Diablo," she said.

"A misnomer, if ever there was one. That horse can barely kick up its hind legs anymore."

"Tell that to my butt," she retorted. "Now back off. The training can wait another day."

"I'm not letting you drag this out forever," he warned her.

"Don't worry about it." She drew a deep breath, then blurted, "If not knowing when we're competing bothers you, I'll set a date. How's the first Saturday after Memorial Day?"

Jake regarded her with astonishment. He wasn't sure which of them was more stunned by the impulsive announcement. "That's less than a month away," he protested.

She gave him one of her saucy grins that had his

stomach clenching and his blood pumping harder. "Then I say you'd better start practicing," she retorted. "After all, you haven't been tossed around by any bulls lately."

"That was not what I meant."

"I'll be ready," she vowed.

"We're not competing until Zeke clears you," Jake countered. "I will not be responsible for you breaking your neck just because you're too stubborn to back down."

"If you'd just sign the ranch over to me, we wouldn't have to compete at all."

"No way, sweetheart."

She shrugged. "Suit yourself," she said, echoing his earlier remark.

Jake smiled grimly. "I always do."

Of course, what would suit him right now would be to throttle Miss Sara Wilde and there was no way in hell he could do that without putting everything he'd worked for at risk. Trent might recognize what a handful his daughter was, but he wouldn't appreciate another man calling her on her behavior.

Unless, of course, that man happened to be married to her.

Two hours into the icy silence that had fallen between her and Jake, Sara realized that she actually enjoyed driving him to distraction. In fact, she'd found the whole morning downright amusing. The frustrated look on Jake's face when he'd realized he couldn't talk her out of coming along had been priceless. He'd appeared cornered, maybe even a little desperate.

That expression confirmed what she'd guessed the night before. He was susceptible to her and he wasn't happy about it. Which meant there might be more than one way to land Three-Stars for herself.

Despite her brave comments on her ability to win their bet, Sara knew that her chances of outlasting Jake on a bronco were slim at best. She needed a backup plan and it appeared that seduction might be its cornerstone. If she could keep Jake off guard and rattled, he might make a mistake that would give her the edge she needed in their competition.

She cast a cautious glance sideways at his harsh profile. With his Stetson settled low on his forehead and his mouth narrowed to a thin line, there was no question about his mood. He was definitely not a happy camper.

Since he'd never reacted so negatively to her presence before, she could only conclude that he suddenly didn't trust himself to be alone with her. That conclusion did wonders for her relatively untested feminine ego.

"Jake?"

"What?"

"Could we call a truce? We are pretty much stuck with each other for the next day or so. We might as well try to be pleasant."

"If you wanted chitchat, you should have gone into town for a visit with your sister."

Sara wasn't about to be put off so easily. "I was just wondering what it was like on the rodeo circuit."

He glanced over at her. "Thinking of taking it up full time?"

She scowled at him. "Hardly. I was just curious."

"I thought I satisfied your curiosity on this particular subject years ago. You pestered me about it enough when I first came to the ranch."

She grinned at him. "I do recall something about ending up polishing your championship buckles."

The hard line of his mouth softened just a fraction. "You were an easy mark."

"I suppose I had a bit of a crush on you back then," she admitted, not sure why she was willing to share such a secret now. Maybe because she'd always thought of Jake as a trusted friend, right up until the moment she'd realized he intended to take what she so desperately wanted.

"I would have done anything to please you," she recalled with a wry smile. "You never took advantage of that, though."

"Except to get you to polish those buckles for me."

She met his gaze. "You know what I meant."

Jake didn't pretend not to understand a second time. "You were a girl, Sara. I may be a low-down skunk when it comes to women, but you were off-limits."

"I'm all grown up now," she pointed out daringly.

He grinned at that. "And more trouble than I can cope with," he told her. "Don't play with fire, Sara. You're liable to get burned."

"That's an odd warning coming from a man who

figures on winning a bet that includes me among the prizes.''

He shrugged. ''I probably should have mentioned the warning before we made the bet. You might not have been so quick to take me up on it. Being married to a man like me wouldn't be any bed of roses. I'm not going to settle down like some docile lapdog, Sara. You ought to keep that in mind.''

''It doesn't change anything,'' she said with a touch of vehemence. ''I want Three-Stars. I'll do whatever it takes to get it.''

''Including making a pact with the devil?'' he asked dryly.

''You don't scare me, Jake,'' she said, surprised by the certainty in her voice. He really didn't frighten her, not nearly as much as he should have, given his coldhearted reputation as a love-'em-and-leave-'em ladies' man. She'd seen exactly how kind and loyal he could be to the people he cared about.

''That's your first mistake, darlin'. You should always be a little bit afraid of a man who controls what you want.''

''You don't control it,'' she shot back. ''Not yet.''

''The papers your father and I signed yesterday say otherwise.''

Sara was so startled by the calm statement, she almost lost control of her horse. Dismay ripped through her. ''You've signed the papers already?''

''You knew we were going to,'' he reminded her. ''It's just a matter of getting the bank's okay on the loan and setting a date for the closing.''

''That can't be. We had a deal,'' she protested. ''I

thought you were going to put everything on hold…''

''I never said that.''

''But I assumed… I thought we had a deal,'' she repeated.

''We do. If by some crazy fluke you win the bet, I'll sign the ranch over to you. If I win, there's no paperwork involved. I keep the ranch and get you in the bargain. Don't count on a big, fancy wedding, though. The very thought of it gives me the jitters.''

Sara wasn't sure why Jake's announcement about the paperwork came as such a shock. She should have known he wouldn't wait for their contest to stake his claim on the ranch. Besides, what would he have told her father about the delay? The truth was certainly out of the question. Her father would go ballistic if he found out about the bet. No, realistically, Jake had done the only logical thing.

A chill washed through her all the same. Once the ranch was in his name, what would prevent him from reneging on their bargain? She believed deep down that Jake was an honorable man, but he was also a man who fought hard for everything he wanted. He wouldn't walk away from what was his easily. And the one thing she had never doubted was that he wanted Three-Stars as desperately as she did.

''Maybe we'd better put our agreement in writing,'' she said.

''Don't you trust me, darlin'?''

There was an odd note of regret mixed in with the amusement in his voice.

"Somebody very wise once told me never to trust a snake not to turn on me," she said.

"Good advice," he agreed. "You draw up your little piece of paper and I'll sign it."

Startled, she stared at him. She'd expected more of an argument. "You will?"

"Why not? I don't have anything to lose."

"Except the ranch," she reminded him.

He shook his head. "Sweetheart, it isn't going to happen. You might as well make a trip into town and have a chat with the preacher. That way you'll have a head start on planning that June wedding. What's the waiting period for a license? Or we could get that now and get married right after you hit the ground."

The shudder that swept through Sara couldn't be blamed entirely on panic. An unmistakable image of an impending wedding night set off a fair share of the trembling reaction she had to Jake's confident words.

He regarded her speculatively. "Unless of course, you've thought better of it and want to call the whole thing off."

"Not a chance," Sara said fiercely, refusing to be provoked into doing what he wanted.

One way or another she was going to have Three-Stars. If marriage to Jake was the only way she could get it, then she'd find some way to live with it.

A surreptitious glance in his direction made her pulse escalate. For some reason she couldn't quite convince herself that having Jake Dawson in her bed would be a total calamity. Maybe it was time she found out for sure.

* * *

How the dickens did she do it? Jake stared across the fire at Sara and cursed his luck for the hundredth time that day. She was sleeping like an innocent babe, while he was tied up in knots.

Leave it to him to develop the hots for a woman as irritating and perverse as Sara Wilde. He'd been in a perpetual state of arousal practically since dawn. Surely a man could die of frustration after a day like that. Tomorrow didn't promise to be one bit easier on his libido.

Meanwhile, Sara had been blithely acting as if she didn't have a care in the world. Even his deliberate taunts about the inevitable loss of Three-Stars hadn't stirred much of a reaction. She'd apparently concluded that the ranch would be hers one way or another and was satisfied with that.

He found her ready acceptance that she might have to marry him to get it a bit disconcerting. He was finally forced to face the fact that he'd gotten himself in way over his head with that impulsive counterbet. There was every chance in the world that he was going to be forced to marry her just to live up to his word.

What in God's name had he been thinking?

He sighed heavily. The truth was he hadn't been thinking at all. He'd reacted impulsively, something he seemed to do all too often where Sara was concerned. Lately his ironclad self-control flew out the window when she was around.

As he was contemplating the reason for that, the distant, plaintive cry of a wolf split the night air. Sara shot upright, which indicated to Jake that perhaps she hadn't been sleeping quite as deeply or peacefully as he'd thought.

"What was that?" she asked.

He didn't buy the startled reaction for a minute. "You've heard wolves before, Sara."

"He sounded close."

"You know how noise carries out here. I'm sure he's miles away. Go back to sleep."

"I don't think I can."

Jake regarded her suspiciously. "When did the sound of a wolf start making you nervous?"

Her gaze met his evenly. The firelight made her eyes glitter like brilliant jewels, the kind of gems that turned honorable men into thieves.

"I guess I'm just jumpier than usual tonight," she claimed. "Would you mind if I moved to your side of the campfire?"

The soft plea put him in a hell of a bind. He might not believe her, but he couldn't very well say no. He'd come off like a hard-hearted jerk. By the same token, saying yes was definitely tempting fate. That campfire was just about the only thing between him and a decision that would lead them both straight to disaster.

"Please," she said softly.

"Come on over," he said, his tone resigned.

Sara slid out of her sleeping bag and carried it over beside his. She spread it out scant inches from him, then wriggled back inside it.

With every shifting movement, Jake's body hummed with awareness. He wanted desperately to slide in her direction, to cover her body with his, to claim her mouth again and prove to himself once and for all if it was sweeter and more enticing than any other mouth he'd ever tasted.

"Jake?"

Jake gritted his teeth. "Go to sleep, Sara."

"I think I'd feel better if you'd hold me."

Sweet heaven, she was going to drive him straight over the brink to insanity. There was no longer a doubt in his mind that she was doing it on purpose, too. Sara Wilde was definitely not the scaredy-cat she was pretending to be. She was one of the strongest, most self-reliant women he'd ever known. Somehow he had to remind her of that.

"Not a good idea, darlin'. Besides, you've been out here at night often enough to know exactly what to do to protect yourself. You don't need me."

"Oh."

That single word was infused with a whole range of emotions— from disappointment to resignation. She sighed heavily.

Silence fell and Jake finally convinced himself that he'd had a narrow escape, but his honor was intact.

"Jake? Are you sure?"

He swallowed hard. "I'm sure."

"Oh."

Maybe it would have ended there. Maybe he would have clung to his fragile willpower for the rest of the night. But that damned wolf picked that precise moment to let out another plaintive howl that, indeed, sounded closer.

Sara was in Jake's arms before he could form a

coherent protest. She was warm and trembling and dangerously provocative with her arms tight around his neck and her face buried against his chest. Her warm breath fanned over his bare throat and turned his blood to liquid fire.

Jake sucked in a deep breath and framed her face in his hands. He leveled a look straight into her eyes. It was possible there was a touch of fear there, but what caught his attention was the blazing awareness, the hunger that surely matched his own.

"Jake."

Her voice was whisper soft and filled with the same kind of longing that echoed what he was feeling. He tried one last time to steel himself against it.

"Shhh, it's okay," he soothed and settled her in his embrace. Every inch of his body fought his attempt to pretend he was simply giving comfort.

Sara shifted slightly until their bodies clung together so intimately that Jake moaned aloud. The last fragile bit of self-control snapped. He moved so quickly that Sara gasped with surprise when she found herself on the ground with Jake poised over her.

"Last chance," he murmured, his gaze fixed on hers.

She responded by pulling his head down until their lips met. Jake couldn't have ignored the invitation then, if Trent Wilde himself had been threatening him with a shotgun.

The kiss quickly turned wicked and desperate. Even as he plundered her mouth with his tongue, even as he savored the sweetness, she was inartfully fumbling with the buttons of his shirt. Her touch on his bare chest made his pulse buck more wildly than any championship bull he'd ever ridden.

Why? echoed through his brain time and again, until he shut off thought and succumbed to pure sensation. The skim of her tentative fingers over bare skin. The moist heat of her mouth closing over a masculine nipple. The silken tangle of her hair brushing across his chest. His entire body throbbed with need. He couldn't recall ever feeling so much urgent hunger.

Counting backward from a hundred, he tried to disengage from the demanding sensations, at least long enough to be sure that Sara was with him, that her body was as ready as his.

It took only seconds to reassure himself. Her skin burned beneath his touch. When he slipped his fingers beneath the hem of her sweater and tugged it off, he discovered bare breasts. The nipples were hard even before he drew first one and then the other into his mouth.

As if from a great distance he heard the soft rasp of a zipper and realized that she was shucking jeans and panties. She bucked and moaned with pleasure when his fingers skimmed intimately over her, sliding deep into damp, welcoming heat.

"Please," she whispered. "Please, Jake. Now."

She was already fumbling with his belt buckle. Jake gently shoved aside her hands and finished the job, shedding his pants in one smooth motion. When he felt her touch on the hard shaft of his arousal, his heart slammed against his ribs.

Why? The question taunted him one last time, but he didn't wait for an answer. It was too late. Nothing could have kept him from taking what Sara so willingly offered. Nothing, perhaps, except a change of heart on her part.

He gazed into glittering green eyes and rubbed his thumb across lips swollen from his kisses. He'd warned her of who he was, just like he'd warned the others. Still, he asked one last time to be sure she understood what she was doing. He wasn't sure if he asked out of honor or in the desperate hope that she would back away and save them both from making what was bound to be a terrible mistake.

"Are you sure this is what you want?" he asked, curling a strand of red hair around his finger, then brushing it gently away from her face. "It's not too late."

His breath seemed to catch in his throat as he waited for her answer. If she said no, if she changed her mind now, he might very well hate himself for the rest of his life for asking. But that would be better by far than having her hate him for not asking.

All she said, though, was, "Please, Jake. Don't stop."

She opened herself to him then. Her hands on his hips guided him. When he would have sunk slowly, carefully into her, she took that option from him, arching her hips until they were joined fully, deeply.

Jake couldn't recall ever fitting another woman so snugly, so perfectly. Nor could he recall a time when his movements had been so tormentingly slow, when the buildup of tension had been so exquisitely consuming.

When a howl ripped through the night air, Jake thought surely it must have been the wolf once more. Then he realized that the sound had come from him just as an explosive climax shuddered first through Sara and then with shattering intensity through him.

He closed his eyes, hoping that would shut out the emotions crowding through him, but it was a wasted effort. Something told him that Sara had claimed more than his body in the past hour. He was very much afraid she had claimed his heart and soul. The real shock, of course, was that he still had either one for her to claim.

Chapter Six

Obviously she'd lost her mind, Sara thought with a
fresh bout of embarrassment as she fought opening
her eyes in the morning. There were fresh reminders
of her middle-of-the-night madness.

Jake's leg was settled across hers. He'd flung one
arm possessively around her waist. His shadowed
cheek rested against her bare shoulder. The intimacy
was beguiling and confusing. When she thought of
how she'd practically—okay, literally—thrown herself at him the night before, it was also humiliating.

Where had she gotten the notion that Three-Stars
could be seduced away from Jake? Just because
she'd proved he wanted her was no reason to assume
he wanted her badly enough to sacrifice the home
he'd dreamed of owning.

Not that he'd tried very hard to fight her off. He'd

put up a token, gentlemanly resistance. It was probably more than most men would have under the circumstances, but he hadn't exactly called a halt to the proceedings.

Which meant one of two things, she concluded. Either he'd been lusting after her as ardently as she'd been lusting after him or he was just the kind of male who never turned down such a generous offer of feminine companionship.

Judging from the rumors about the trail of broken hearts Jake had left behind, it was more than likely the latter.

She went back to the original question. What the devil had possessed her to fling herself at him? She tested a few more theories, hoping she'd like them better.

Maybe she had just wanted to discover whether their marriage would be more than compatible in one respect. That was a good one. Logical even. Not even Jake could argue with it. In fact, he'd already embraced that very concept when he kissed her the first time.

Or maybe all those years of pent up longings had finally gotten to be too much to resist. She wasn't as crazy about that one, but unfortunately it made a lot of sense. All that taunting talk of marriage had finally encouraged her to take matters into her own hands.

Or maybe she really was naive and foolish enough to figure she could seduce Three-Stars away from him. Stupid, stupid, stupid! There was no getting around it. That was a game she couldn't possibly win.

Whichever motive it was, she had clearly wandered onto dangerous turf. While it was true enough that she might hold some power over Jake when it came to sex, she'd also discovered that his hold on her was just as powerful. She didn't need a map to know that big-time trouble lay at the end of that particular path.

Since he hadn't moved in some time, she dared a peek at him. The sight of raw masculinity that greeted her gaze took her breath away. She'd always known he possessed a magnificent body. She'd even seen the rippling muscles in his shoulders and arms before as he worked around the ranch bare chested in the summer heat. But the combined effect of tapered waist, lean hips, muscular legs and stirring arousal slammed through her like a freight train.

Humiliation and embarrassment be damned! She wanted him again, wanted him with a hunger that stunned her. When had she turned into such a shameless hussy? If she wasn't careful, she was going to allow this consuming need for Jake Dawson's body to cloud her thinking. She needed all her wits about her if she was going to hang on to the ranch. That was her number one priority and she couldn't lose sight of it.

With careful deliberation, she shimmied out from under him, alert for any sign that he was awake and not just having one heck of a hot dream.

She was almost free, when his arm snagged her waist and pinned her in place.

"Going somewhere?" he inquired in a lazy, sexy tone that rippled over her.

"It's dawn," she improvised, feigning a carefree cheerfulness she was far from feeling. "We've got work to do."

"It can wait," he insisted, his hand possessively cupping her breast. He skimmed the nipple with his thumb, sending shock waves all the way to her toes.

"Oh, no," she insisted breathlessly. "We have to stay on schedule."

He regarded her curiously. "Why the sudden worry about deadlines?"

"I have an appointment with Zeke later today, remember?"

"How could I forget?" He grinned impudently. "Don't worry. I can make sure this won't take long. We'll get you back in plenty of time."

Sara scowled at him. "How romantic of you."

His expression turned serious. "Romance has nothing to do with anything happening between us," he assured her. "We're talking about steamy, mutually satisfying sex."

Sara figured she deserved that. She was the one who'd practically pleaded with him to make love the night before. It was hardly any wonder that he'd gotten the idea that she would go along with a hot, no-strings affair. Still, it hurt hearing him say that it had meant nothing more to him. That was yet another warning that what had happened couldn't be repeated.

She forced a nonchalant shrug. "Last night was a mistake. There's no need to repeat it."

Surprisingly, Jake stilled. "A mistake?" he asked, his tone lethal.

His demeanor radiated a warning, but Sara was too intent on escaping with at least a shred of pride intact to pay any attention to it.

"Everyone's entitled to one, right? I'm sorry if you got the wrong idea." She leapt up and grabbed her clothes. "I'll be ready to get to work whenever you are."

She dashed through the underbrush to the nearby creek and splashed herself thoroughly with very cold water. It chilled her skin, but did nothing at all to cool her temper or her desire.

Still, by the time she returned to the campfire, she managed to appear outwardly calm. Jake's grim expression suggested he was in as much turmoil as she was. He gestured toward the pot of coffee.

"It's hot, if you want some."

Sara nodded, took her cup out of her saddle pack and poured some of the rich coffee into it. She had a feeling, though, that mixing caffeine and her already jittery nerves was a very bad idea. When Jake held out one of Annie's blueberry muffins, she accepted it, careful to avoid so much as grazing his fingers.

"Maybe we'd better talk about what happened here last night," Jake said eventually.

"I thought we had discussed it," Sara retorted stiffly. "What more is there to say?"

"You could tell me why you threw yourself at me in the first place."

She shot him an icy look. "Excuse me?"

"You know that's what happened."

"If that's what your monumental ego needs to believe, go ahead,'' she snapped as fresh humiliation rushed through her.

"It's the gospel truth. I'm just wondering what was behind it.'' He regarded her intently. "Or don't you know?''

Sara finally dared to look directly into his eyes. Rather than the smug amusement she'd expected, she found only genuine bemusement, maybe even genuine concern. She sighed. Perhaps honesty was the answer.

"I have no idea,'' she admitted eventually. "One minute I was half asleep, the next minute I heard that wolf and all I could think about was having your arms around me. It didn't make a lick of sense to me then and it doesn't now. Then one thing led to another so fast, my head was spinning.''

Jake did grin at that. "There are some things in life that defy explanation,'' he conceded. "I suppose we could chalk this up as one of them.''

Sara drew in a deep breath. "I promise it won't happen again.''

Something that looked very much like disappointment shadowed his eyes. "Too bad,'' he murmured. "I can't help thinking something that spectacular shouldn't be wasted.''

Hearing Jake voice the very regret that had been ricocheting through her head all morning startled her. But she wasn't the kind of woman who made love willy-nilly just because it felt good. Last night had been an aberration, not the start of a very bad habit. Or so she hoped.

"I think we'd better forget all about last night," she insisted.

"Easier said than done, sweetheart."

Sara prayed that Jake was wrong about that. If she couldn't forget how close she'd come to finding heaven in his arms, how would she ever say no to him again?

Sara's lesson with Zeke was a disaster from the moment she first climbed into the saddle that evening. Her concentration was shot and her muscles felt like limp noodles. She'd never been more grateful that Jake had insisted on riding broncos, rather than bulls. A bull would probably have bounced her from here to Montana by now.

The third time she slammed into the ground, her bones rattled so hard she was astonished they didn't shatter. Zeke's expression was thoroughly disgusted as he hauled her to her feet again.

"Enough," he said. "We're just wasting time and risking that pretty neck of yours today."

"We can't stop," she pleaded. "I told Jake I'd be ready by the Saturday after Memorial Day."

Zeke's muttered curse blistered her ears. "Why'd you go and do a damned fool thing like that?" he demanded.

"He was getting impatient. He won't wait around forever."

"He'll wait until I say it's okay," Zeke said grimly. "So will you. Now git on into the house and tell Mary Lou I said to give you a cup of tea and some of her special liniment."

Sara started to protest, but Zeke had already turned his back and headed for the barn. He didn't appear inclined to listen to any arguments.

Groaning as she dusted herself off, she resigned herself to following instructions. All of this docile obedience was beginning to grate on her nerves. Unfortunately, she needed Zeke's help too badly to tell him off.

Limping, she crossed the yard to the back door. It swung open the minute she set foot on the porch. The cheerful, round-faced woman with soft brown curls who greeted her was a surprise. She'd expected Zeke's wife to be as pinch-faced and ill-tempered as he was.

"Oh, you poor little thing," Mary Lou soothed. "Come on in here this minute. I've already got the tea brewing. How about a nice slice of coconut cake to go with it? Or maybe you'd prefer some hot biscuits with fresh-churned butter and homemade strawberry jam? You need to put a little meat on those bones if you're going to be tossed on your backside half a dozen times a day."

She urged Sara toward a seat at the big round oak kitchen table. Fortunately, the chair was padded with bright yellow cushions. Sara wasn't sure she could have handled a hard wooden seat just then.

Since she'd never responded to the various food choices Mary Lou had offered, Sara was startled when a plate filled with biscuits and a huge slice of cake was plunked in front of her, along with a pretty glass dish of jam.

"Eat what you can," Mary Lou said, bustling

around with the kind of spry energy that accomplished a lot in very little time. "Don't worry about anything going to waste. This place is crawling with birds and animals just waiting for scraps. Zeke says they're the real reason I cook so much food."

As if to prove the point, a low-slung hound dog inched out from under the table to take up a hopeful position at Sara's feet.

"Ignore him," Mary Lou advised. "He's an unrepentant beggar who'll take your whole meal if you let him."

Either she was hungrier than she'd realized or she was rising to the challenge of competing with that sad-faced hound dog for the food on her plate. The next thing Sara knew she'd eaten every crumb and finished her third cup of tea.

Mary Lou beamed at her. "There's more if you want it."

"No, please. That was plenty. I can't thank you enough. I feel almost human again."

"No need to thank me." She regarded Sara slyly. "Of course, you could tell me about this bet between you and Jake. Zeke won't say a word and Jake just grumbles when I ask him. I'm dying of curiosity."

Maybe the food had made her mellow. Or perhaps she'd just been longing for a friendly ear. At any rate, the next thing she knew, Sara was spilling out the whole story of her desperate bid to keep the ranch she loved.

"Oh, my," Mary Lou clucked more than once as Sara talked.

"The bottom line," she concluded, "is that I have

less than a month to get ready for this contest. If today is any indication, I might as well forget all about it now."

"Oh, piddle," Mary Lou said. "It's way too soon to give up. Exactly what does Zeke have you doing?"

As Sara described the step-by-step attempts to improve her skills, Mary Lou plagued her with detailed, surprisingly astute questions.

"You sound as if you know this business as well as your husband," Sara said finally.

"Oh, I suppose I even know a thing or two he doesn't," Mary Lou said with an enigmatic little smile. "But don't tell him I said that." She shook her head. "I just can't help thinking, though, that it might have been wiser to choose a different challenge. Jake never lost a rodeo competition."

"Don't remind me," Sara said with a sigh. "But it was all I could come up with in a hurry. I figured he was too much of a gambler to turn me down and I was right."

Mary Lou looked thoughtful. "Of course, he did send you to Zeke. Clearly he wanted to give you a fighting chance. I wonder why."

"Probably so he wouldn't have to feel guilty if I killed myself."

"I don't think so." She surveyed Sara intently. "Is there something you haven't told me about this bet?"

Sara thought of Jake's insistence that she become part of the prize if he won. She hadn't mentioned that to Mary Lou. "Actually, there is one thing," she said slowly. "If he wins, he gets to keep the ranch...and me."

Mary Lou's eyes widened. "Oh, my." Then she started to chuckle. "Well, if that don't beat all."

"What?"

"Jake's made it plain ever since I've known him that he has no intention of marrying. I wonder why he'd make that part of this particular bet?"

"I think it was an impulsive decision on his part. He was hoping to scare me off," Sara admitted for the first time.

"But you didn't run scared, did you?" Mary Lou observed. "Surely he knows you well enough to have guessed you wouldn't. Jake must be downright terrified about now. Talk about being caught between a rock and a hard place. If he loses the bet, it'll cost him the one thing he's always wanted, that ranch of your daddy's. If he wins, he'll have to do the one thing he's always sworn he'd never do."

Mary Lou grinned approvingly. "Sounds to me as if you have that man exactly where you want him."

It sounded more to Sara as if that crevice between the rock and a hard place was getting crowded. From her perspective, it appeared there were two of them in there.

The only things on Sara's mind when she finally got back to Three-Stars were a hot bath, a rubdown with some of that liniment Mary Lou had given her and a long night's sleep. Naturally since she was feeling very much frayed around the edges, her father had other plans for her. He intercepted her as she was trying to slip quietly up the back stairs.

"Where the dickens have you been, girl?" he demanded with a disapproving scowl. "We have company coming for dinner in twenty minutes."

Sara practically groaned aloud. "Not tonight, daddy. I'm beat."

"That's not my problem. If you'd been home where you belonged, you'd be rested. If you hurry, you can manage a quick shower. It'll fix you right up."

"These are your guests," she protested. "You can entertain them. You don't need me."

Her father's jaw set stubbornly. "They're our guests," he corrected. "I invited the Pattersons just so you and Harold could get better acquainted."

Sara did moan at that. "Daddy, talking to Harold Patterson is about as scintillating as watching prairie grass grow. I guarantee you that I'll fall asleep before we get through the appetizers."

The threat didn't seem to overly alarm him. "I trust the good manners your mother taught you will prevent that from happening," he said dryly. "Twenty minutes, Sara Jane. I won't be kept waiting."

Sara had two choices. She could ignore her father's edict and risk his wrath or she could show up, be polite for a few minutes and then claim a violent headache. In truth, the latter wouldn't be a lie. Just the thought of conversing with dull Harold Patterson for several hours was enough to make her head pound.

Obviously, her father wasn't content to try to manipulate Dani's life. Now he was determined to meddle in Sara's as well. Clearly it was going to take some fancy footwork to avoid falling in with his plans, but with any luck she and Dani could hold out until he was safely off in Arizona. Open defiance might very well delay his departure. Feigned obedience was probably the smarter tactic.

With that in mind, she showered and dressed in a pair of tailored beige slacks and a rust-colored silk blouse. The outfit was dressy enough to pass a fatherly inspection, but hardly likely to give Harold ideas. Not that Harold ever had any ideas that she'd noticed.

Downstairs, she found the Pattersons and her father gathered in the seldom-used living room. An expectant silence hung in the air. Her entrance brought a flurry of conversation, which amounted to little more than inquiries about everyone's well-being and an all-too-brief discussion of the weather, which everyone agreed had been unseasonably warm that afternoon.

When silence fell again, Harold's gaze settled on her so hopefully that Sara couldn't help wondering exactly what her father had said to the man. Knowing Trent Wilde's old-fashioned notions, she wouldn't be surprised if he'd dangled the promise of a generous dowry in front of him.

"How's the boot business?" she asked eventually. The Pattersons—father and son—made fine leather cowboy boots just as preceding generations had before them. They were very good at what they did, which made boots about the only topic of conversation at which they excelled.

"We made four pairs special order for a big actor out in Hollywood," Harold said.

"Oh, which one?" Sara asked. For once she didn't have to fake enthusiasm. She loved movies.

His expression went blank. "I don't recall. I haven't seen a movie in years." His face brightened. "But he wanted the very best leather." He launched into a detailed dissertation on the making of the boots that had Sara trying to desperately stifle a yawn.

When footsteps sounded in the hallway, she glanced up gratefully. Hopefully Annie had dinner on the table, which would mark the beginning of the end of this disastrous evening.

Instead, she found herself gazing straight into very familiar, taunting blue eyes. Despite her resolve to resist Jake Dawson, her pulse skittered crazily.

"There you are," her father said heartily. "Come on in, Jake. We've been waiting for you. You know the Pattersons."

Jake made the same mistake Sara had. He asked about the boot business. The entire story of the Hollywood-destined boots was repeated with mind-numbing detail. Even the ever placid Mrs. Patterson looked bored to tears by this time.

Jake accepted a drink from Trent, then made his way straight to Sara's side. When he settled onto the love seat next to her, she suddenly felt crowded. Though his attention remained dutifully focused on the other guests, his outstretched arm rested a scant inch or so from Sara's shoulders. His heat seemed to surround her. Before she could adjust to that alarming sensation, his fingers skimmed the back of her neck.

The first fleeting touch might have been accidental and innocent, but the lingering caress that followed was deliberate and wicked. Sara's pulse bucked and the evening turned into a whole new challenge. Rather than worrying about falling asleep, she had to worry about falling under Jake's spell for the second time in two days.

She cast a quick, panicked glance at the others to see if they were aware of Jake's subtle, sensual assault, but everyone's attention appeared riveted on Harold, who was describing yet another pair of boots he'd designed for a famous country music star. Naturally, he didn't know the singer's name, only his foot size. Harold would clearly never be leaking gossip to Liz Smith or "Entertainment Tonight."

By the time Annie finally announced dinner, Sara was certain that Jake was the most devious, despicable man she'd ever known. He knew perfectly well that she couldn't make a scene in front of the others. Worse, he probably knew that those sneaky caresses were the only thing standing between her and total boredom. He probably even considered it his duty to drive her wild and, thus, keep her awake.

As they moved toward the dining room, Harold formally offered Sara his arm.

"I was delighted when your father suggested this dinner," he said to her as Jake looked on with blatant amusement. "It gives us an opportunity to get reacquainted. I'm looking forward to hearing what you've been doing with yourself lately."

Jake's guffaw of laughter at that had Sara's cheeks flaming. She turned and shot a fierce warning look in his direction. Harold glared at him with apparent annoyance and leaned down.

"I can't imagine why your father included the help tonight," he murmured.

The comment snapped the last of Sara's patience with the whole, ridiculous evening. "You must not have heard," she replied in a silky sweet undertone. "This is Jake's home now. My father is selling Three-Stars to him."

She wasn't sure who was more disconcerted by her announcement, Harold because it destroyed his image of her as one of the heiresses to the ranch or Jake because she'd made the statement without the slightest trace of venom. She was beyond caring if her father discovered she knew about his plan. Let the whole lot of them go straight to hell.

Jake recovered first. "Of course, Sara will stay right here as long as she likes," he chimed in, then added, "One way or another."

Harold looked confused by the enigmatic remark. "I don't understand."

Sara patted his arm. "Don't worry about it. Jake and I have a little bet going about the future."

"Perhaps it's good that we came tonight," Harold said solemnly. "I'm sure there's an alternative for your future that you haven't considered. We can discuss it after dinner, if you like."

Jake winked at her. "See, Sara. Your options are unlimited."

"Oh, go to hell," she muttered under her breath.

She was sure, based on his amused expression, that Jake heard her. Unfortunately, so did Harold. His shocked reaction made her wonder if he was already having second thoughts about proposing to a woman who couldn't control her tongue.

Please, heaven, let that be the case, she thought desperately. If Harold Patterson actually put a formal proposal on the table, her father would have her marching down the aisle before she could explain that she had stupidly gone and fallen in love with another man.

Something told her that Trent Wilde might be happy to sell his ranch to Jake Dawson, he might even enjoy including him in an occasional dinner party, but he might not be nearly so content to have the rogue rodeo champ as a son-in-law.

Boy, was he in for a shock, if their bronc-riding contest turned out the way Jake obviously intended it to. It would almost be worth losing, just to see the look on her father's face when he discovered she'd made her own rather unorthodox arrangements for her marital future.

Chapter Seven

Jake couldn't recall the last time he'd enjoyed one of Trent Wilde's stuffy little dinner parties more. The Pattersons were nice enough people, but about as entertaining as waiting for a bone to heal, something with which he had all too much experience.

As for placid, insipid Harold Patterson, he was no match for a woman of Sara's quick wit and energy. He'd bore her to death in a week, maybe even on their wedding night.

If the Pattersons had been dull dinner companions, Sara's presence had more than made up for them. In fact, tormenting sweet Sara had removed the slightest trace of tedium from the evening. She was so readily rattled, so easily stirred by the slightest, most innocent touch. He'd thoroughly enjoyed making her cheeks flame and her pulse race with the sneaky caresses she couldn't acknowledge or fight off.

Unfortunately, he'd had to suffer the consequences—another very long, very restless night. With the memory of another far more exhilarating end to an evening fresh in his mind, his body ached like the very devil.

By morning he was exhausted and cranky. He was in no mood to hear from Zeke before dawn. For Zeke to use the phone at any hour could only mean trouble. Jake was in no mood to deal with trouble either.

"What the hell are you calling about?" he snapped.

"You're going to have to put an end to this lunatic bet of yours," his friend announced without preamble.

Jake moaned. "Zeke, I am not talking about that now. Call me back at a civilized hour. It's my one day off and I was planning to sleep in."

"If you'd buy one of them fancy-schmancy answering machines like everyone else in the whole dang world, I wouldn't have to call you back at all," Zeke retorted, undeterred by Jake's plea. "I could have left a message the first time I called last night. Or the second. Or the third."

"I thought you hated answering machines even more than you do phones."

"They're the devil's own invention, but by midnight last night when you still weren't home, I was beginning to grasp the fact that they have their uses."

If Zeke had made that many attempts to reach him, Jake concluded, then this nonsense about canceling the bet was serious. Portable phone in hand, he reluctantly rolled out of bed and paced the room trying to wake up. The icy floor pretty much jolted him into an alert state.

"Maybe you'd better start at the beginning," he suggested mildly.

"Beginning, middle, end, it don't make no difference," Zeke retorted. "Like I said, the bottom line is you've got to call off this bet."

"Why?"

"Because Sara has no business trying to ride a bronco," Zeke said succinctly. "She like to broke half her bones yesterday. Another couple of lessons and it's my guess she'll be in casts from head to toe. I've got Mary Lou nagging at me to boot. She's been fussing like a mother hen. She thinks I'm going about this all wrong. She's been picking at me all night long about the techniques I'm using."

Jake muttered a string of obscenities he rarely used. "What the devil does Mary Lou have to do with this?" he asked eventually.

"To my everlastin' regret, she and Sara had a nice, long chat yesterday."

Jake gritted his teeth. "How did that happen? Dammit, Zeke, I told you to keep 'em apart."

"Never you mind how it happened," Zeke responded irritably. "The point is, now Mary Lou's worried about her, which means I ain't going to have a minute's peace until you call this off. Mary Lou's going to be dogging every move I make and telling me what I should and shouldn't be doing. I won't have it. I work alone. Always have." He heaved a put-upon sigh. "It's up to you to end this."

"It is not up to me," Jake corrected. "The bet was Sara's idea."

"Maybe so, but I've seen the way her eyes light up when your name's mentioned. You've got more influence with her than I have. Besides that, no one I know has a better reputation as a silver-tongued devil. Surely you can sweet-talk her into giving up, if you put your mind to it."

"And just what would you suggest I tell her?"

"You'll think of something," Zeke said confidently. "You always do."

Jake grasped at one last straw. "You could just refuse to give her another lesson."

"And disappoint her?" Zeke sounded downright horrified by the idea. "Not me. I feel too bad that she's in this fix in the first place. Between you and that daddy of hers, she's getting cheated every which way."

"What do you intend to do if she shows up for another lesson?"

"I'm counting on you to see that doesn't happen."

"And if I fail?" Jake persisted, knowing Zeke would have a backup plan.

"Okay, just in case, I'm thinking of taking Mary Lou down to Denver for a couple of days," he admitted.

"Isn't that a little cowardly, even for you?"

"I call it a strategic retreat," Zeke claimed. "Besides, Mary Lou's been wanting to do some shopping, maybe go to the theater. Maybe that'll get her mind off Sara's situation and her mouth off my case."

"You hate shopping and the theater," Jake reminded him.

"Not as much as I hate thinking of the look I'll see in that gal's eyes if I'm the one to send her packing," Zeke said grimly. "I'm warning you, though. I can't stay away more than a day or two. I'm trusting you to take care of everything before I get back."

He hung up before Jake could ask if he could join Zeke and Mary Lou in Denver. He pretty much knew what the answer would have been anyway.

After the call, Jake dreaded running into Sara. No matter how he sliced it, she was going to be devastated if the bet was called off. He wondered just how inept she was at riding. She must be awful if Zeke had given up after just two lessons. Knowing him, those lessons had been on the tamest horses he owned that qualified as broncos.

"You certainly look gloomy," Annie observed when he wandered into the kitchen for a cup of coffee. "What's wrong?"

"Nothing."

"I know nothing when I see it," she countered. "And this isn't it. The deal for the ranch hasn't gone sour, has it?"

Jake shook his head. "Not the way you mean. It's just that there are a few complications I hadn't anticipated."

"Financial complications?"

"No, nothing like that. Look, I don't want to talk about it, okay?" To escape the questions, which he sensed were far from over, he poured himself another cup of coffee and headed for the door. "If anybody needs me, I'll be in my office."

"Since when do you go outside to get to your office, when you're already in the house and could go straight through the dining room?" Annie demanded. "Never mind. I can guess. When you don't want to run into Sara."

She poked a spoon covered with pancake batter squarely into the middle of his chest. "I warned you, Jake Dawson. I told you to stay away from her. What have you gone and done?"

Jake dabbed ineffectively at the dribbles of batter on his shirt. "Let it be, Annie. Just let it be."

Naturally, she couldn't. At least, Jake assumed that was why Sara herself wandered into his office not five minutes later carrying a plate of hot cinnamon rolls. She looked about as thrilled to be there as he was to see her. Prisoners facing a life sentence were undoubtedly more cheerful.

"Annie sent these. She said you didn't eat any breakfast."

"I wasn't hungry."

Sara stared at him in disbelief. "My heaven, is the sky falling, too?"

"Very funny. Okay, you've done your duty, you can go now."

He realized too late that the dismissal was bound to stir a rebellion.

"Trying to get rid of me?" she inquired. "What a difference a few hours makes. Last night, you couldn't seem to keep your hands to yourself."

The unexpectedly teasing reminder stirred Jake's senses right back to the fever pitch that had kept him awake all night. "But old Harold's not here this morning, so what would be the fun in it now?" he retorted.

"So your only intention was to irritate him?" Sara asked, her expression skeptical.

Jake shrugged. "What else?"

"I thought perhaps you were trying to stake a claim for yourself."

"Why would I want to do that?"

"Why do men do anything?" she asked with a shrug. "Possessiveness. Machismo. Whatever you want to call it."

"Sorry to disappoint you," he said blandly. "But goading Harold was the only sport I had in mind."

Sara didn't seem to believe him. In fact, she was heading his way with a very determined gleam in her eyes.

Before he could guess what she had in mind, she'd scooted his chair away from the desk and plunked herself squarely into his lap. Her mouth covered his before he could ask her what the devil she was up to. After that, any questions he might have had flew straight out of his head.

She tunneled her fingers through his hair and brushed tantalizing, lingering kisses across his forehead, his cheeks and his chin before finally zeroing in on his mouth again.

She was wearing some sort of provocative, musky scent that reminded him of sex. Jake wasn't nearly strong enough to resist that kind of temptation.

He figured he'd better savor these last few kisses, because once he told her Zeke's edict, it was very likely she was going to break something over his head. It would probably mark the last of the kisses, too.

In the past week or so Sara had discovered something about herself, something she never would have suspected. She was a very brazen woman. She was quite adept at this flirting stuff. She'd always assumed that Ashley was the only one who'd gotten a full measure of that particular gene. She and Dani had always been the sedate ones by comparison to their youngest sister.

Now, as she savored yet another of Jake's devastating kisses which she had initiated, she was feeling very much a woman of the world. She was also only about one spine-tingling brush of his lips away from hauling him onto the floor for another passionate session of lovemaking.

Given his moodiness when she'd first walked into the room, maybe she ought to wait on that until she had some idea what had happened between last night and this morning. Satisfied that he was in an improved and definitely more attentive frame of mind, she pulled away with a contented sigh.

"Much better," she murmured, skimming a finger across his lips. His eyes darkened at her touch.

"Better than what?" he asked suspiciously.

"That scowl you were wearing when I walked in. What was that all about, by the way?"

He hemmed and hawed for several seconds, before finally admitting, "I had some bad news earlier."

Sara stilled at his suddenly somber expression. "Is it something you want to talk about?" she asked sympathetically.

"Not particularly, but I suppose now's as good a time as any to tell you."

"Me? It has something to do with me?"

He nodded, but that was about as forthcoming and revealing as a generic newspaper horoscope as far as she was concerned.

"Specifically?" she encouraged.

Jake looked as if he'd rather eat dirt than tell her. "Zeke called," he said eventually, then stopped again.

"And?" she prodded.

"He wants to call off your lessons."

It took several seconds for the blurted response to sink in. When it did, fury streaked through her.

"He wants to do what?" She stood up at once and backed away. Indignation joined anger and rippled through her at this low-down, sneaky turn of events. She studied Jake's expression, then accused, "You're making that up. Zeke didn't say a thing to me about canceling my lessons."

"That's because he's a coward," Jake said, looking very put-upon. "He insisted I be the one to tell you."

"I don't believe you."

Jake shrugged. "Go ask him yourself, but you'd better hurry. He was planning a trip to Denver so he'd be gone in case I didn't pass along the bad news."

"You put him up to it, didn't you?" she charged. "You set me up with him, then told him to cancel out so we'd have to call off the bet."

"I did no such thing."

His voice rang with sincerity, but Sara was in no mood to believe anything that came out of his lying mouth. "Well, let me tell you something, mister," she said.

She jabbed a finger into his chest, which she noticed seemed to be coated with odd little patches of dried pancake batter. If she hadn't been so mad, she might have pursued how they'd gotten there. Something told her it would be a fascinating story. In the meantime, though, she had a point to make.

"I do not intend to call off this bet," she told him vehemently. "If Zeke won't teach me to ride, then you'll just have to do it yourself."

"Oh, no, you don't," he said, holding up his hands in a no-way gesture. "I'm not about to give lessons to my own competition. Besides, if Zeke says you have no business riding a bronco, then I'm the last man in the world who'd argue with him."

"How convenient for you," Sara snapped. "Well, don't go counting your chickens just yet, Jake Dawson. When I get finished with Zeke Laramie, he'll be begging me to stay on as his student."

Jake's lips twitched at that, but Sara was beyond caring. She was going to hold Zeke to their deal if she had to use every ounce of influence she possessed. She hadn't been raised by Trent Wilde for nothing. She knew exactly how to throw her weight around when she had to. It wasn't a tactic she enjoyed, but desperate times called for desperate measures.

She was halfway out the door, when Jake called after her. Only the oddly gentle note in his voice kept her from ignoring him. She faced him slowly.

"What now?"

"I really am sorry about this."

"I'll bet," she said. "No need to worry, though. It's just a temporary inconvenience. We'll be back on track before the end of the day." She forced a smile. "Or you can kiss this ranch goodbye right now. If I tell Daddy the bet you agreed to, he'll cancel your deal so fast that the eight seconds you used to stay on a bull will seem like an eternity."

Jake's shaken expression told her that he knew as well as she did that Trent Wilde would not be happy to discover that Jake had been willing to let Sara risk her neck to claim Three-Stars.

Only she knew, though, that it was an idle threat. She didn't want her father drawn into this. He'd made his choice. If she got the ranch now, it had to be because she'd earned it on her own, even if her methods were a little unorthodox.

A half hour later, her anger mounting, she was squealing to a halt in Zeke's driveway. Just to prevent a quick getaway, she parked her car so that it blocked his pickup.

She marched around to the back door and pounded on it so hard, it shook on its hinges.

"Okay, okay," Zeke grumbled as he limped

slowly into the kitchen. "No need to knock the house down. I heard you." When he recognized her through the screen door, he turned pale. "Oh, it's you."

"Darn right, it's me," Sara said, pushing past him. Hands on hips, she leveled a look straight into his eyes. "Mind telling me why you're calling off our lessons?"

He looked everywhere but at her. "Jake told you, then."

"I didn't get it by divine messenger, that's for sure. So, what's the deal?"

"You haven't got what it takes," he said bluntly.

"You mean you haven't got what it takes to teach me," Sara countered.

"If it makes you feel better to think that, it don't bother me none. Bottom line, you ain't got no business trying to ride a bronco."

The plainspoken assessment shook her as nothing else could have. She didn't want to believe it, so she tried blaming it on Jake's influence. "Is that your honest evaluation?" she asked skeptically. "Or did Jake plant the idea in your head?"

Zeke didn't appear to take offense. "I've got eyes and sense," he said. "I don't need Jake to tell me what's plain as day."

"Well, I am going to ride a bronco," Sara retorted adamantly. "Now I can do it with or without your help. If you don't help, then more than likely, I will be seriously injured, maybe even killed."

She allowed that to sink in, then added, "Without Three-Stars, nothing much matters to me anyway."

Zeke regarded her with obvious horror. "Don't you ever say a thing like that. That's pure craziness."

"It's the way I feel," she insisted stubbornly.

Zeke scowled at her, then gestured toward a chair. "Sit down. Maybe we should talk this through."

Sara stood right where she was. "There's nothing to talk about. Either you're willing to help me or you're not. Which is it?"

"Mary Lou ain't going to like it," he muttered under his breath.

"This is between you and me," Sara argued. "Your wife doesn't have anything to do with it."

"That's easy enough for you to say. You don't have to listen to her twenty-four hours a day."

Sara decided the hardball tactics had taken her as far as they were likely to. She moved in for the kill.

"Zeke, please," she pleaded. "I don't have anywhere else to turn. If you don't help, that ranch is as much as Jake's. Is that fair? Shouldn't I at least have a fighting chance to keep what should have been mine in the first place?"

Before Zeke could answer, Mary Lou walked into the kitchen carrying a suitcase. She took one look at Sara and sighed deeply.

"I suppose the trip to Denver's off," she said to Zeke. She didn't sound particularly surprised about it.

Zeke shot a disgruntled look at Sara, but nodded. "We'll go for a whole week in June," he promised. "Right after this danged fool bronc-riding contest."

Sara breathed a sigh of relief. "Thank you." She gazed at Mary Lou. "I'm sorry about the trip."

Mary Lou shrugged, eyes suddenly twinkling. "Never even packed," she said, indicating the suitcase. "Zeke never could resist a lady in distress. But as worried sick as I was about you, I had to try. When push came to shove, I knew he wouldn't be able to let you down."

She put a hand on her husband's shoulder and squeezed. "I do think there might be an alternative, though. Zeke's used to teaching men. Maybe you ought to be getting your lessons from a woman."

Zeke and Sara both stared at her in astonishment.

"A woman?" Sara said, just as Zeke muttered something that sounded like, "Well, I'll be damned."

"Who?" Sara asked.

"Me, of course," Mary Lou said briskly. "Time was when I could outride half the men on the circuit, Zeke included. That's how we met."

Sara's eyes widened. "And you'd be willing to teach me?"

Mary Lou patted her cheek. "Honey, I know tricks this man couldn't begin to guess. If you're determined to go through with this, you might's well be taught by the best."

To Sara's surprise, Zeke didn't look the least bit insulted by his wife's claim of superiority. In fact, his eyes were shining with pride.

"Are we agreed, then?" Mary Lou asked.

Zeke nodded. "It makes sense to me. What about you, Sara?"

"I'm flabbergasted, but yes, of course." She

glanced suspiciously at Zeke. "Unless that means you're going to be sneaking off now to coach Jake."

Zeke hooted at that. "Jake doesn't need coaching. Nope, you're going to be getting two for the price of one now, that is if Mary Lou will let me put my two cents in every now and again."

His wife grinned. "Could I stop you?"

"Not likely, any more than I could stop you from taking over once you saw how determined she was."

Sara glanced from Zeke to Mary Lou and back again. "You planned this to happen, didn't you?" she asked him.

"Me?" he said innocently. "I was ready to call the whole thing off."

"So you say," Sara retorted.

"However it happened," Mary Lou said, "the point is that time's flying by and we've got work to do. You ready for another lesson, Sara?"

Sara nodded. "Let's do it." She grinned. "I can hardly wait until Jake hears about this turn of events. When I left the ranch this morning, I'm sure he was convinced he had this little contest all locked up."

"Of all people, Jake should know it ain't over 'til it's over," Zeke said, grinning. A glint of pure devilment lit his eyes. "I sure would like to be there when he finds out I lured Mary Lou out of retirement for this gig."

"Then why don't the two of you join us for supper tonight," Sara suggested impulsively. "Jake promised me a dinner for helping him with the books the other day. I think tonight's the perfect time for him to pay up."

Zeke and Mary Lou exchanged an amused and suspiciously knowing look.

"You're on," Zeke said.

"This promises to be more fun than my last rodeo championship," Mary Lou agreed.

Sara had to admit she was looking forward to it, too, but probably not for precisely the same reasons. She'd just grown increasingly addicted to spending time with one ornery rodeo cowboy.

Chapter Eight

Sara was in a very strange mood, Jake concluded, watching her meander around his office, a secretive little smile on her face. For the life of him, he couldn't get a fix on how things had gone at Zeke's.

She didn't look distraught, so maybe she had succeeded in persuading Zeke not to abandon her. He wasn't sure he wanted to know how she'd accomplished that. He already knew that Sara's unexpected wiles added up to a dangerous weapon.

"What's on your mind?" he asked eventually.

"I was just wondering if you were busy tonight?" she asked, carefully avoiding his eyes.

"Why?"

"You promised me dinner if I solved that little bookkeeping problem the other day. You haven't paid up."

"Sorry. A few things came up."

"I'll say," Sara said under her breath.

Jake doubted she intended the remark for his ears, so he swallowed the irreverent laugh that bubbled up in his chest. She had a way of taking him by surprise that was thoroughly disconcerting. Even though he was suspicious of her motives, he couldn't resist this latest opportunity to find out what she was up to now.

"Tonight's fine. Where do you want to go?" he asked.

"How about the Old West Grill? They have country-western dancing tonight. I feel like kicking up my heels."

Jake got the distinct impression there was more on her mind than whirling around a dance floor, but he'd made her a promise. It was too late to back out on it now just because he'd envisioned something slightly more private and romantic.

"Seven o'clock," he suggested.

"I'll be ready."

Ready for what, he wondered. Something in her tone suggested to him that there was a warning there he shouldn't ignore. For the life of him, though, he couldn't figure out what was going on in that pretty little head of hers.

Maybe that was why he couldn't seem to shake the almost constant thoughts of her. She was like a missing word in a crossword puzzle, nagging at him to find a solution.

Unfortunately, no answers came to him. He still didn't have a clue about what she was up to when he pulled up in front of the main house at seven.

Sara slipped out the door before he could set foot on the front porch, which suggested to him that she didn't want her father to know about their plans for the evening. For some reason that grated on him. It reminded him all too plainly that for the time being he was nothing more than a worn-out rodeo champ and Sara was the daughter of the prominent and powerful Trent Wilde.

He resisted the almost overwhelming desire to march inside and announce that he and Sara were going out for the evening. There really was no point in stirring up that particular hornet's nest just for the momentary satisfaction of seeing Trent's shocked expression.

Instead, he focused on the woman who'd slipped into the car beside him. He surveyed the slim-fitting jeans that cupped her incredible derriere, then moved on to the western-cut shirt that molded itself to her breasts, and the boots that emphasized her shapely calves. With her red hair spilling over her shoulders in sexy disarray, she was enough to turn a saint into a sinner. No one had ever considered Jake to be a saint. Pure lust hammered through him.

"If you aren't the prettiest sight I've seen in a long time," he told her. "I'm going to be the envy of every male in the Old West."

"I suppose that will make your day," she retorted.

He grinned at her. "Compared to the rest of the day, it won't hurt."

As they drove into town, a comfortable silence fell in the car. Jake was surprised that Sara didn't see any need to fill it with idle chatter the way a lot of women would. It was yet more proof that Sara wasn't like other women. He should have found that satisfying, but for some reason it only scared the daylights out of him. It reminded him he was up against an unpredictable force. Bull riding had been unpredictable, too, but he'd mastered that. He told himself he could master Sara, if he tried hard enough.

What startled him even more than his determination to figure out this hold she had on him was how much he enjoyed not just her astonishing sensuality, but simply her company. He'd always assumed the only way for a man to guarantee any peace and serenity in his life was to keep a woman out of it. Sara was proving to be an exception to that.

"You going to get around to telling me what happened at Zeke's today?" he inquired eventually.

"Maybe later," she said.

"Still too upset to talk about it?"

"Not exactly."

The answer was a little too enigmatic to suit him. "You'd probably feel better if you'd just get it out of your system. Go on and yell, if you feel like it," he said generously. "I won't hold it against you."

She actually grinned at that. "I don't think yelling would accomplish anything, but thanks for offering."

"What will help?"

"A good dinner, pleasant conversation, some dancing," she said. "That and the company, of course."

"I'll do my best to cheer you up," he promised, though for some reason he couldn't fathom, she didn't seem all that upset to begin with.

"Don't worry, I won't put all the burden on your shoulders."

He regarded her curiously. The comment suggested she had plans for tonight that he knew nothing about. If she intended to torment him by dancing with every man willing to give her a spin around the floor, then she was in for a big surprise. Jake never shared. With his background, it hadn't been a trait he'd learned. He saw nothing particularly admirable about starting now with Sara.

He was still mulling over her comment, when they walked into the already smokey, crowded interior of the Old West. He was about to suggest that Sara wait while he circled the room in search of a table, when she latched on to his hand and pointed across the dance floor.

"Over there."

"You see an empty table?"

"No, Zeke and Mary Lou. They're saving one for us."

A tingle of dread slithered down Jake's spine. That old familiar crowded feeling crept over him. "You knew they were going to be here?"

"Sure. I thought it would be fun to get together with them. You're old friends, right?"

"Right," Jake agreed tersely. At the moment, however, he was viewing Zeke as being a whole lot closer to a traitor, than a pal. The fact that Sara was still so chummy with him suggested that the lessons were on again. No wonder she was in such a terrific mood. She'd won another battle of wills. The victory must be tasting sweet about now.

Zeke stood up as they reached the booth. Jake shot him a sour look, then smiled at Mary Lou and leaned down to kiss her. It wasn't her fault she'd hooked up with a dirty, rotten scoundrel.

"You're looking more beautiful than ever, darlin'."

"And you're every bit as handsome as ever," Mary Lou replied. "It must be a trial being so good-looking. Do women ever want you for your brains?"

"I wouldn't know. I don't waste time asking," he countered just as he always did.

Mary Lou shot a look toward Sara, then said pointedly, "Maybe it's time you did."

"Okay, you two, enough," Zeke grumbled. "Sit down. I'm starved. I've ordered ribs and beer. Hope that's okay."

Since there was very little else on the grill's menu that was worth discussing, Jake nodded. People didn't come here for the food. They came for the music and the noise and the camaraderie.

Jake let Sara precede him into the booth, then slid in next to her, close enough to be sure she wouldn't be able to ignore his presence.

After one quick, amused glance, she countered his move, by making sure they were hip to hip and thigh to thigh.

Check and checkmate.

Jake leaned back and surveyed his three companions thoughtfully. "Okay, what's up?"

Three innocent gazes met his. Mary Lou's were the first lips to twitch with amusement. He leaned across the table and tucked a finger under her chin.

"Okay, you. What's up?"

"Who says anything is up?" she replied, smiling sweetly.

"I didn't just fall off a turnip truck, darlin'. You all look like a trio of cats that've been feasting on plump old canaries."

They didn't even have the decency to look guilty. Jake waited, but when not a one of them opened up, he tried again. "Should I assume from the way you're acting that the riding lessons are on again?"

"Oh, definitely," Sara said as if there'd never been any doubt about it at all.

Jake shot a look at Zeke. "No willpower, huh?"

"Well, she was mighty persuasive," he agreed, "but I'm not the one who's going to be teaching her." He nodded toward his wife. "Mary Lou is."

If Jake hadn't spent a lifetime learning to disguise his feelings, his mouth would have dropped wide open. Mary Lou hadn't been near a rodeo ring since she'd retired. He'd only seen her ride once, but the experience had been memorable. He'd always regretted that their paths hadn't crossed sooner, so he could have watched her in her prime. She had epitomized all of the flowery descriptions of those riders who were at one with their horses, a single unit of grace and passion and power.

"Well, well, well," he murmured. "Sara must have made quite a case for herself to drag you out of retirement."

"Let's just say I'm sympathetic with her desire to hold on to what's hers," Mary Lou responded tartly.

"And I do look forward to someone bringing you down a peg or two."

"And you think Sara can do that?" Jake asked.

"I'd stake one of Zeke's prize horses on it."

"Oh, no, you won't," Zeke replied heatedly. "I don't want my horses mixed up in this foolishness."

Jake slanted a look at Sara to see just how much she was enjoying all of this. Her smile suggested she was very pleased with herself. That smile was pure challenge as far as Jake was concerned, as much of a dare as if she'd spoken aloud.

After listening to be sure the music was slow and provocative, he leaned over and whispered, "Care to take a whirl around the dance floor, sweetheart? You did say you wanted to kick up your heels this evening."

The dare in his invitation was unmistakable and they both knew it. Her startled gaze met his. The smile trembled on her lips before fading. As the sensual beat of the music registered, she swallowed hard, then shrugged.

"Sure, why not?" she said, her voice satisfyingly breathless.

Grasping her hand in his, he helped her from the booth, then promptly spun her into his embrace. Her body fit perfectly against his own, too perfectly for comfort.

Jake recognized his mistake instantly. Even the slightest contact with Sara had the power to arouse him. With her breasts snug against his chest, her hips molded to his and her thighs brushing his each time they swayed to the soft music, his entire body was on fire.

And so, he realized, was hers,

He might have taken some satisfaction in knowing that she was as hot and needy as he was, but it was difficult to get past his own aching yearning to strip away clothes and pretense.

Never in his entire life had a woman gotten under his skin so immediately and so effectively. Given his determination to avoid emotional entanglements, it terrified him.

But he was willing to overlook the fear. The feelings were too fascinating to ignore. Some perverse, daring, analytical part of his brain wanted to figure out why the chemistry between them was so explosive.

"Jake?"

"Hmm?"

"The music's stopped."

He gazed down and discovered amusement mixed with awareness in her eyes. He grinned impudently and tightened his embrace ever so slightly. He swayed with her to an unheard beat.

"Is that a problem?" he asked, his eyes locked with hers.

"It's not a problem for me, if it's not for you," she said bravely. "We are attracting just the tiniest bit of attention, though."

"Darlin', I've been a sucker for attention ever since I rode my first bull into the ring and heard the applause."

Defiance flared in her eyes. "Then by all means,

let's give them something to look at," she said and
twined her arms around his neck.

Lifting herself on tiptoe, she slanted her mouth
across his in a no-holds-barred kiss that flat out left
Jake weak-kneed. No woman ever had had that kind
of power over him, not even that heartbreaking Sue
Ann.

When Sara finally pulled away, he stared at her,
dazed. "You are a very dangerous woman, Sara
Wilde."

A grin of absolute delight spread across her face,
as if he'd just confirmed her own discovery.

"And I'd advise you not to forget it," she said,
slipping from his embrace and sashaying back to the
table in a way that had Jake's blood pumping harder
than a Texas oil rig.

Up until now, Jake had thought he was in control
of whatever was happening between him and Sara
Wilde. The last few minutes had proved otherwise.
For a man who never, ever, let his control of a situation slip, the realization was damned disconcerting.

All of her life Sara had run to Dani with her prob-
lems. Something told her, though, that her big sister
wouldn't have the answers she needed to deal with
Jake. For this, she needed the advice of an expert in
the battle of the sexes. That meant Ashley.

Ashley had dated more boys in Riverton than all
of the other girls in her class combined. Sara had no
reason to think she wasn't cutting an equally wide
swath through the bachelors in New York. She was
pictured in the tabloids with a different man on her

arm practically every week, though none got more than a casual mention in her letters or calls home.

Ashley adored men. She reveled in their attention, but she would never let a man interfere with achieving her goals. Sara prayed her sister could give her some tips for maintaining that same focus when she was in Jake's powerful presence.

It was after midnight in Wyoming when Sara dialed her sister's number. Except when she had a crack-of-dawn photo shoot, Ashley was a night owl. Even with the time difference, it was unlikely she was asleep, and if she was, she never minded being awakened for some girl talk.

Sure enough, she answered on the second ring, sounding as alert as if it were two in the afternoon, rather than two in the morning.

"Is this the world famous cover model?" Sara asked.

"Depends on who you ask," Ashley retorted. "What on earth are you doing up at this hour? I thought you got up with the chickens."

"We don't have chickens," Sara reminded her tartly. "You should come home more often. You'd know that."

"Okay, who's the man?" Ashley asked, ignoring the pointed jibe about her unfamiliarity with the operation of Three-Stars.

The accuracy of Ashley's guess was irritating. "Man? Who said anything about a man?" Sara demanded.

"That's the only thing I can think of that would

keep you up this late and cause you to call your baby sister at this hour."

"Maybe I just wanted to hear the sound of your voice."

"It's Jake, isn't it?"

The direct hit left Sara speechless. Ashley hadn't even seen her for months now. Had she always been that obvious about her feelings for the ranch foreman?

"What's he done to you now?" Ashley persisted.

"Why would you think this has anything to do with Jake?" Sara asked.

"Because not one single man other than Jake Dawson has caught your eye since the day he showed up at Three-Stars. Sooner or later, all that longing was bound to erupt. What happened? Did you finally lose control and make a pass at him?"

Trust Ashley to cut to the chase. "You could say that."

"Well, hallelujah!" When Sara remained silent, Ashley quickly took the hint. "Uh-oh, did he reject you?"

"Not exactly."

"Oh, my."

"Oh, my, indeed," Sara said fervently.

"How far has it gone?"

"That's personal."

Ashley chuckled. "That far, huh? So, what's the problem? You should be in heaven. Or wasn't he all you'd anticipated?"

"Oh, no, he was exactly the way I'd imagined he would be."

"So?"

"I'm playing in the big leagues and I'm afraid I only have minor league skills," Sara blurted.

"Which naturally made you think of me," her sister said dryly. "Thanks a bunch."

"Come on, Ash, you've never let a man tie you up in knots. You stay cool and calm and collected no matter what."

"Is that supposed to flatter me? Maybe that's because no one like Jake has come along for me."

To Sara's surprise, Ashley sounded wistful. "What about that guy, the one back in high school that no one knew you had a thing for?" she asked.

"I can't imagine who you mean," Ashley said in a defensive way that suggested she remembered every detail.

An almost forgotten image promptly came to mind. Sara described what she recalled. "Dangerous. Rebel. Sexy. I believe those were just a few of the words associated with him. Miss Perfect and the bad, bad boy. It always had a nice ring to it, if you ask me."

The laughter that greeted her comment sounded a little forced. "You have a wild imagination, big sister," Ashley protested.

"No, I have a long memory. Tell the truth. Are you regretting the choices you've made?"

Her sister sighed. "No, modeling was my ticket out of Wyoming. It's been very good to me." She hesitated, then added, "At least up until now."

"Meaning?"

"Meaning nothing," Ashley said, suddenly brisk

and businesslike. "You didn't call to talk about me. Let's figure out what to do about Jake."

Sara wasn't about to be put off so easily. "You know this giving advice stuff cuts both ways. I may not know much about the modeling business, but if you need to talk, I can certainly listen."

"Thanks, but this is one problem I have to resolve on my own."

Sara seized on the slip. "Then there is a problem."

"Drop it, Sara," Ashley ordered impatiently. "Now tell me exactly what you're worried about with Jake."

Pestering Ashley with more questions was obviously going to be a waste of time. Sara forced herself back to the reason for the call. "I'm worried that I've gone and fallen in love with him," she said.

"And that's bad?" Ashley asked, not sounding the least bit surprised by the admission.

"It is, when Jake has done everything but spell it out in skywriting that he positively hates the idea of marriage."

"It's men like that who end up falling the hardest," Ashley said. "Give him time."

Of course, in time, it was true that they could wind up walking down the aisle, Sara conceded to herself. Their bet might assure that, but Sara knew with every fiber of her being that Jake had never meant his impulsive proposal to be taken seriously. Now it hovered over them like some sort of dark and threatening cloud.

She sighed. She couldn't tell Ashley any of that. It would mean getting into all of the hurt and betrayal she'd felt when she discovered their father's plans for Three-Stars.

"Can you make a man fall in love with you?" Sara inquired wistfully.

"You can't make a man do anything he's set against," Ashley said. "But you can be patient and loving and understanding, so you're the one who's there the day he wakes up and decides it's time to get married. If the chemistry's there, you've definitely got a jump start on the process."

"Patient, loving and understanding?" Sara echoed. "What about just plain driving him to distraction?"

Ashley laughed at that. "Better yet. You don't need advice from me, sweet pea. If you're driving Jake to distraction, it sounds like you're doing just fine on your own."

"Don't say anything about this to Daddy or Dani, okay?"

"We made a pact years ago to protect our secrets from Daddy's meddling. As for Dani, I haven't spoken to her in weeks now."

"How come?" Sara asked, then guessed the answer before Ashley could reply. "She's too good at seeing through you, isn't she? She'd know right off that you're worrying about something and you don't want to get into it, right?"

"Goodbye, Sara. Good luck with Jake. He's a lucky man."

"Ashley Wilde, don't you dare hang up on me."

The edict came too late. Sara heard the phone click before she could complete the sentence. She could call back, but she knew that Ashley would only let the phone ring unanswered.

Of the three sisters, Ashley appeared to be the most open, the most outrageous, the most unflappable. But Sara knew better. Her younger sister was the most private, the most mysterious and the most vulnerable of all of them.

That night the memory of Ashley's unspoken pain vied with Jake for Sara's thoughts as she drifted off to sleep. But once her dreams began, it was no contest. Jake was at the center of every one.

Chapter Nine

For the next week Jake drove himself until exhaustion took over and numbed his mind. It was the most effective way he could think of to keep his growing feelings for Sara from luring him into doing something he'd regret.

Unfortunately, he hadn't come up with any way at all to keep her out of his dreams. She plagued him like the very dickens from the minute his head hit the pillow and his eyes closed. She didn't let up until he dragged himself awake in the morning, exhausted and disgruntled.

Why Sara? He asked himself that over and over again. Of all the women he'd ever known, why had she been the one to nag at him like a tantalizing, once-familiar scent?

She was lovely, but so were dozens of others.

She was sexy, but he'd never been drawn to the demure type. His relationships—if they could be called that—had all been blatantly sexual.

Was it as perverse as the fact that she'd always been so far out of his reach? Surely he was too old to be wanting a woman just because he couldn't have her. Besides, Sara was hardly unattainable. She'd made her availability abundantly clear and he'd happily taken advantage of it.

For some reason he couldn't fathom, it wasn't enough. He wanted more, but he couldn't put a name to the unfamiliar yearning.

After a week of denying himself the pleasure of seeing her, of touching her, he realized that abstinence wasn't doing a darn thing except to put a more demanding edge on his need.

He told himself it was only curiosity that drew him to Zeke's place late one afternoon when he knew Sara would be there for her riding lesson. But the truth was, the minute he laid eyes on her straddling a very restless bronco in the chute, his heart slammed against his ribs and then wound up in his throat.

He wanted to yell to Zeke not to open the gate. He wanted to go over and haul Sara off the back of the horse and cradle her in his arms, but he did neither of those things. He stood in the shadow of the barn and watched while Sara bent down to listen to a last bit of advice from Mary Lou, then smiled confidently.

"Let's do it," she told Zeke with gumption to spare.

Damn, but she was fearless, Jake thought. Normally, it was a quality he would have admired, but at the moment, it didn't seem like a particularly admirable trait.

The gate opened, the bronco shot into the ring, bucking and twisting to rid itself of the annoyance on its back. It didn't take three seconds to send Sara flying into the air. She landed with a thud in the dust, disgust written all over her face. If she was in pain, she ignored it.

"How long?" she demanded.

"Two point three seconds," Zeke told her.

"Damn."

"That's longer than last time," Mary Lou consoled her. She draped a comforting arm over Sara's shoulders. "Now here's where you went wrong."

Her voice dropped to a confiding level that prevented Jake from hearing what she had to say. He realized that his hands were clenched into fists and his heartbeat had slowed to a dull thud.

It was worse than he'd thought. Sara just wasn't cut out for bronc riding and all the lessons in the world weren't going to change that.

Unfortunately, no one would be able to get that message across to her. She had too much riding on trying to best him. Determination, desperation and pride would force her not to accept the only rational advice: that she drop out now.

"You saw?" Zeke asked in a low voice.

Jake hadn't even heard him approach, hadn't even realized that Zeke had noticed him in the shadows. "Every agonizing second," he told him.

"I'll give her one thing, she's got heart."

"A lot of good that'll do her, if she gets herself killed," Jake retorted. "What am I going to do? I can't let her take this kind of a risk."

"You don't have any choice," Zeke said. "Not unless you aim to turn Three-Stars over to her without a fight. I'm not even sure she'd accept that. She wants that ranch in the worst way, but she wants it on her own terms. That's plain enough. She's got something to prove, to you, to that fool daddy of hers, maybe even to herself."

Jake shook his head. "Well, I've got to come up with something." He met Zeke's worried gaze. "Don't tell her I was here, okay?"

"Not a chance. Knowing you'd seen her would be worse humiliation than taking that fall. She's gotten to taking those in stride," he added dryly.

The frightening image of Sara slamming to the ground stayed with Jake all the way home. He shuddered every time he thought about it. Yet not one single, solid idea for avoiding tragedy came to him.

Even so, he found himself watching for Sara to come back from Zeke's. Maybe he'd be struck by some brilliant answer once he laid eyes on her.

Instead, the only thing that struck him as she limped out of her car and headed wearily toward the house was how badly he wanted to drag her into his arms and hold her. Maybe take her into his place and run a hot bath for her to soothe her aching muscles, then rub her down with some of Mary Lou's special liniment.

And, then? Well, it probably wasn't smart to go imagining what might follow. He leaned back against the fence rail and struck a match to light a cigarette. Despite his intentions to quit, there were times when nothing matched drawing that smoke deep into his lungs.

The tiny spark of the match apparently caught her attention as surely as if he'd turned on a pair of high beam headlights. She turned his way.

"Jake?"

"Hey," he called back softly. "Rough day?"

She made a valiant attempt to straighten up and put a little spring into her step. His admiration for her fierce determination grew.

"No rougher than the rest of them," she said.

Jake suspected that was the gospel truth. "It won't be too much longer. You sure you're going to be ready?"

"Absolutely," she insisted.

There was a cocky, confident note in her voice that he recognized as pure bravado.

"There'd be no shame in calling things off."

She shook her head. "I can't," she said simply. "It's the only chance I have."

Jake knew all about only chances. He'd spent a lifetime grabbing on to them to haul himself out of the morass that had been his childhood. Owning Three-Stars was yet another one of those, perhaps the last and most rewarding yet.

Recognizing that the ranch was just as important to Sara and knowing that it put them forever at odds came closer to breaking his heart than anything that had ever happened to him.

He met Sara's bleak expression and felt the sudden, surprising sting of tears. What the hell was happening to him? Nothing had moved him to cry in years.

Maybe if he'd been a different man, he could have given Sara her dream and walked away to find another one for himself. It would be the right thing to do, the noble thing.

But his own dreams had been tied up in Three-Stars for too long. He couldn't see beyond it to any other possibilities.

That meant one of them would win and one would lose. With stakes that high, it seemed unlikely that the loser would ever forgive. No matter which of them came out the winner, Three-Stars would stand between them, as impenetrable a barrier as any fortress ever built.

And that struck Jake as almost unbearably sad.

Standing next to Jake with the first shimmering rays of moonlight cutting through the night sky, Sara was almost certain she saw the sheen of tears in his eyes. But, of course, that couldn't be. A man like Jake never cried, never even acknowledged his emotions, as far as she could tell.

Unable to stop herself, she lifted her fingers to his cheek and touched dampness. Proof positive that something of enormous import had happened. Even as she wondered what on earth it could be, Jake shuddered and stepped away.

"Jake, what is it?" she pleaded, stunned.

"Nothing, just a little dust in my eye, that's all."

Sara didn't believe him, but knew that pursuing it

would cost them both. She accepted the lie. Lying to cling to pride had gotten to be second nature to her lately. Jake had the same right.

"Want to go inside, so I can check it out? I have some eye drops."

"Nope. It's better already."

She slanted a devilish grin at him. "Okay, then, how about just going inside?"

She thought she detected a muscle working in his jaw. He seemed to be struggling with himself. When he finally lowered his gaze to meet hers, his eyes were glittering with unmistakable desire.

"Your place or mine?" he asked, in what sounded to be part jest, part very serious question.

"Before I answer that, will you tell me something?"

"If I can."

"What's going on between us?"

A slow grin began to tug at his lips. "Darlin', if you don't know the answer to that, maybe you shouldn't be playing the game."

"Exactly," she said vehemently. "Is that all it is to you, a game?"

"A very grown-up game," he said.

Swallowing back the hurt that the cool reply stirred inside her, she asked, "Care to share the rules with me?"

Jake suddenly looked vaguely uneasy. "No rules, just instinct."

"Whatever that means," she snapped. She studied him thoughtfully. "Jake, don't you ever get tired of games? Don't you ever wish that everyone would just lay all the cards on the table and be direct? Haven't you ever wanted just to be with someone who cared about you without any pretenses, without any emotional barriers?''

He muttered a curse and dropped his cigarette, crushing it beneath the heel of his boot. "You've been reading too many fairy tales," he replied. "In real life, there are always pretenses and lies."

A chill seemed to settle over Sara's shoulders. He believed that. She could see the bleak acceptance of it in the harsh lines of his face.

Before she could stop herself, she reached up and traced the downward curve of his lips. His skin heated beneath her touch. Sparks flared in his eyes.

"This is real," she whispered. "The way you respond when I touch you is real, Jake. Surely, you believe in that."

When he remained perfectly still and silent, she took his hand and guided it to her breast. "Can you feel the way my heart is pounding right now? That's real. No pretense. No lie."

She felt the shudder that ripped through him, heard his soft moan in the instant before he hauled her into his arms and crushed her mouth beneath his.

Sara had no idea if he understood what she'd been trying to say, if he even cared. She knew only that he wanted her with a desperation that matched her own. No pretense. No lie.

In fact, each time they kissed, the heat burned brighter and hotter than before. No one, not even the very cynical Jake, could deny the truth of that.

"Yours," she whispered, her breathing ragged.

"What?" Jake murmured, his expression bemused.

"You asked before whether we should go to your place or mine," she reminded him. "I want to go to yours." In case that wasn't emphatic enough, she added, "Now."

Jake hesitated for the space of a heartbeat, his gaze searching her face for something. He must have found what he was looking for, because he nodded.

He had just folded her hand in his and started off toward the foreman's cottage, when the front door opened, spilling light and shadow across the lawn. Sara knew without turning that her father stood framed in the doorway. Dismay flooded over her.

"There you are," Trent said. "I thought I heard voices out here. Sara, I've been looking for you."

She cast a look of regret at Jake, then turned. "Oh? Any particular reason?"

"Annie was wondering if you planned to be home for supper. I didn't have an answer for her." He glanced at Jake. "Why don't I tell her to set the table for three? Jake, you'll join us, won't you?"

Jake was starting to shake his head, when Sara squeezed his hand. "Please, Jake. Join us."

He looked as if he'd rather be caught in a blizzard, but he forced a smile. "Sure. I'd be a fool to turn down Annie's cooking."

Trent gave a nod of satisfaction and went back inside to pass along the word to Annie, leaving Jake and Sara alone.

"You do like to play with fire, don't you, sweetheart?" Jake inquired.

"That's a given, *sweetheart*." Sara beamed at him. "Besides, a little delayed gratification is good for the soul."

"It's not my soul I'm worried about," Jake said dryly.

"Maybe you should be."

"At the moment, I have more pressing matters on my mind," he told her. He moved her hand to the front of his jeans. "See what I mean?"

Desire ricocheted wildly through Sara. Only an image of her waiting father dampened it. "If you hurry, I suppose there's time for an icy shower before dinner," she said considerately.

"Only if you intend to share it with me."

"That would more or less defeat the whole purpose, wouldn't it?"

"If the purpose is to do something about my little problem, then I can almost guarantee having you with me would do the trick."

She grinned at him. "You are bad, Jake."

"And you love it," he guessed.

"You are broadening my horizons, that's true."

"Glad to oblige."

"I'm sure."

The taunts might have gone on if Trent hadn't bellowed from inside, "Get on in here, you two. Annie's got supper on the table."

"So much for that shower," Sara said with regret.

"That'll teach you to waste time talkin', when we could be doin'," he responded, winking at her as they went inside. "I surely do hope your daddy is a less observant man than I always took him to be."

It was the longest, most tedious dinner Sara had ever sat through. She couldn't look at her father for fear he'd guess what was on her mind. She couldn't look at Jake, because he knew darned well what was on her mind. As for concentrating on dinner, it might as well have been sawdust for all it mattered to her. She made an effort to at least note what was on her plate, so she could compliment Annie on it later.

Was she turning into some sort of sex-starved wanton? Or was it just Jake and the fact that she'd been falling in love with him since the first day she set eyes on him? The last few weeks had been a dream come true.

What they had right now might not last. In fact, if Jake had his way, it probably wouldn't. That made these hours and days all the more precious. She couldn't have walked away from what he was offering if she'd wanted to.

She was so lost in her thoughts that she almost missed her father's announcement to Jake that the bank had promised to set the closing on the ranch for the following week. Naturally he didn't spell it out in front of her, since she was supposed to be in the dark on the plans, but the enigmatic remark he made was clear enough for her to interpret it.

If she hadn't figured it out on her own, the quick, worried glance Jake shot at her would have been enough to clarify it. She feigned a sudden fascination with the untouched mashed potatoes on her plate in the hope that neither of them would see the tears shimmering in her eyes.

When she had herself thoroughly under control,

she pushed her chair back from the table. "If you two will excuse me," she said cheerfully, "I have some calls to make before it gets to be too late. I'll say good-night now."

She rushed from the room before either of the men could say a word to stop her.

In her room, she shed her clothes and jumped into the shower, an icy one she hoped would cool the angry thoughts coursing through her.

It was all slipping away even faster than she'd expected. The closing would make the loss of the ranch real, no matter what happened after. It would be the official signal that her father truly didn't understand her at all.

Up until now, she supposed she had harbored some slim hope that he would wake up and come to his senses before the deal was finalized. The last of her illusions had been wiped out at the dinner table tonight. Getting Three-Stars for herself really was going to be up to her.

Her spirits sank even further as she thought about the disastrous lesson she'd had that afternoon. She'd been fooling herself about having any chance at all against Jake. Even though the eventual outcome was all but certain, she would go through with the challenge, because she had to.

And if Jake won, as expected? Would he really hold her to the marriage? She doubted it. The dare he'd made had just been part of the diabolical game he liked to play. She was certain he never intended to claim her.

But what if he did? Could she go through with it?

Their conversation earlier tonight merely confirmed what she'd known all along. Jake didn't trust anyone except himself. What kind of marriage could two people have, if there was no trust? How could she bear to be tied to a man she loved, knowing that he didn't love her?

"Damn them both," she muttered, then added for good measure, "Damn all men."

"Your mood's certainly taken a nosedive," Jake commented lazily.

Sara's startled gaze flew to the mirror, where Jake's reflection stared back at her. She tugged the towel she was wearing a little tighter and prayed the steam would hide her flaming cheeks.

"How the hell did you get in here?" she demanded.

"I knocked. I guess you didn't hear me."

"I was in the shower."

Jake's eyes glittered dangerously. "I thought we were going to do that together."

"I don't think so."

"Changed your mind, huh? I suppose I have your father's little announcement to thank for that."

She thought she detected a note of sympathy in his voice. That grated on her nerves almost as badly as his intrusion into her room.

"Don't waste time feeling sorry for me," she said. "It's a little hypocritical under the circumstances."

She glanced over her shoulder and added, "I think you'd better get out of here before my father figures out where you are."

"Your father's gone into town," he said, a note of triumph in his voice. "A poker game, I believe."

"Oh," she said, suddenly sounding a little too breathless. She found the instinctive reaction extremely irritating. "I still think you should go."

"That's your trouble, darlin'. You use your head too much. Stop thinking and tell me what you really want."

"I really want you to get the hell out of my room," she insisted stubbornly, praying he wouldn't see through the blatant lie.

Naturally he didn't pay the slightest bit of attention to her. Even as she waited for him to go, she saw him move slowly forward, one lazy, insolent step at a time. She could feel his heat even before he slid his arms around her waist from behind. When his lips brushed the back of her neck, she weakened.

When his hands slipped past the edge of the towel to cover her breasts, the last of her resolve melted away. The reflection in the mirror as the towel slid to the floor turned her knees to jelly.

"Damn you," she muttered, but without much vehemence.

It was the last thing she said for a long, long time. She turned in his arms and lifted her lips to his.

Tomorrow would just have to take care of itself, she thought, as she gave herself up to the intensity of his caresses. All that mattered was here and now. No pretenses. No lies.

Chapter Ten

Jake slipped out of Sara's room before dawn. He wasn't sure if he was more terrified of being caught by Trent or by Annie. Neither of them was likely to cheer this incredible, unexpected affair he was having with Sara. Trent's aim with a shotgun was lethal, but Annie was capable of doing significant damage with a mere broom, to say nothing of the way she wielded kitchen utensils.

To his amazement, he discovered that for the first time in his life he was worrying about disappointing people he cared about and admired. At the same time, the very real risk of getting caught added an element of danger and excitement that heightened all of the other emotions he was feeling.

And what a mix they were. Sara enticed him and baffled him. She was surrounded by enough warning signs to scare off men far more intrepid than he was and yet, he ignored them, just like he ignored the alarms that went off in his head every time he got close to her.

He wasn't used to being so out of control, to feeling so much desire that nothing else in the world seemed to matter...including Three-Stars.

He knew in his gut that he was putting the ranch at risk every time he slept with Sara. If Trent discovered the affair, Jake could kiss their deal good-bye. And still, he had stolen into her room under Trent's very own roof and made sweet, passionate love with her all through the night. He hadn't waited five minutes after Trent had left for town before sneaking up the stairs to take up where they'd left off when her father had interrupted them earlier.

Was he deliberately trying to blow the deal? Was he consciously putting his own dream at risk so that Sara would somehow realize her dreams without his having to make the actual sacrifice? He was perverse enough to do something like that, but he could honestly say he didn't have a clue about his real motives. He simply couldn't stay away from her.

And the helplessness that that implied did scare him, more than Trent, more than Annie, more than the prospect of losing the ranch.

He'd almost crept out of the house to safety, when a hand snagged the back of his collar and jerked him to a halt.

"Not so fast," Annie said, hauling him around to face her with so much force Jake practically skidded on the just polished kitchen floor. Annie wasn't a big woman—barely five-five and a hundred and twenty pounds, he guessed—but fury gave her unexpected strength.

The room was still dark, but light spilled out of Annie's quarters just beyond. She was still wearing her robe and a fierce expression that warned him not to argue with her.

When she pointed him in the direction of the table, he grimaced, but he dutifully sat. He felt an awful lot like a kid trapped in the principal's office awaiting the verdict on his fate. He'd spent a lot of time under just such circumstances before he'd quit school and run off to chase the rodeo. It had been years before he'd accepted the foolishness of his actions and managed to get his degree.

Before he could wander too far down that particular memory lane, Annie snapped his attention back to the present.

"You didn't pay a bit of attention to me, did you?" she demanded, glowering at him. "You went right ahead and started messing with that girl."

Jake prided himself on not being a kiss-and-tell man, even when the facts were plain as day. He regarded her blandly. "I have no idea what you're talking about."

Annie rolled her eyes in disbelief, but spelled it out just in case. "You and Sara, that's what."

"What about us?"

His persistent vagueness simply irritated her. She shot him a look of pure disgust. "Jake Dawson, I wasn't born yesterday. You spent the night with her. Don't even try to deny it."

"I was in my office," he swore, not entirely certain if he was trying to protect Sara's honor or save his own hide. "Fell asleep at the computer."

"That's funny. You weren't in there when I checked the doors right before I went to bed last night."

Through the years Jake had grown very adept at verbal tap dancing. He didn't even hesitate. "I came over in the middle of the night. I couldn't sleep."

"But staring at that old computer screen did the trick. Knocked you right out," she said with obvious derision. "Come on, boy, you can do better than that."

In the face of Annie's continued skepticism Jake finally gave up. "No, I can't. That's it. Take it or leave it."

To his surprise, Annie's face crumpled. She sank down heavily across from him. "Why, Jake? Why Sara, of all people? There are dozens of women in town who'd fall all over themselves for a second glance from you. Why did you have to pick on Sara?"

Her bleak tone and worried expression got to him as her cross-examination had not. "I wish to hell I knew," he said honestly.

That earned him a faint smile. "Well, well, well," she murmured thoughtfully. "If you can admit a thing like that, maybe there's hope for you, after all."

He regarded her suspiciously. "What's that supposed to mean?"

"I think maybe I'll let you try to figure it out on

your own," she said. "Now go on home before Mr. Wilde comes down to see what's going on. I can't lie to his face the way you can bend the truth to mine."

She had relented so quickly, it made his head spin, but Jake recognized a near miss when he saw one. He leaned down and kissed Annie's cheek. "Thank you."

"Don't go thanking me. I expect you to do some hard thinking. If I don't like the answers you come up with, I won't hesitate to go to her father with what I know. I owe him that, after all these years."

"Just how long is this reprieve going to last?" Jake asked curiously.

"Until I say it's over," Annie responded. "I wouldn't take too long, if I were you, though. The older I get, the less patience I seem to have."

"Is that it or are you still a sucker for a happy ending?" Before she could reply, his expression sobered. "I'm not sure a happy ending is possible here, Annie."

"Sure it is," she said with more confidence than he felt. "I have faith in you."

"That makes you one of the few."

"Along with Mr. Wilde and Sara," she retorted. "Think about that, why don't you."

Jake thought about little else the rest of that day and the next and the next. If there was an answer to Annie's riddle, he couldn't find it. Or maybe he just didn't like the one that kept coming back to him: marry Sara. Forget the bet. Forget his own vehement opposition to marriage. Forget everything except the love that shone in Sara's incredible emerald eyes every time he touched her.

Could he believe in that? Nothing in his life had prepared him for the possibility that love really did exist. Years of doubting couldn't be wiped out with good sex and a gentle smile.

So he continued to fight it. He kept his distance from Sara, too. It was too hard to think straight when she was close. He'd accused her recently of thinking too much. Now the tables had turned. He couldn't seem to stop thinking. Round and round in circles his thoughts went, reaching no conclusions, just tormenting him with unanswered questions.

When he couldn't stand it any longer, he headed into town for an evening alone at the Old West Grill. He'd foolishly figured that the night out would put some perspective on the strange new feelings tormenting him. He counted on a glance into another pretty face stirring his blood as it always had. Wouldn't that just prove that this thing with Sara was as temporary as every other relationship he'd ever indulged in?

He'd been at the bar for an hour now. Three women he'd dated in the past and one he'd never met before had approached him with willing smiles and smoky, seductive voices. He hadn't felt so much as a flicker of awareness, much less the throbbing desire that had once been second nature.

Staring sourly at the line dancers, he took his first long, slow swallow of beer. It was already warm. He was in deep trouble. No doubt about it. He couldn't even drink worth a darn.

"You look like a man with a lot on his mind," Zeke noted, sliding onto the stool next to him.

"Give it a rest," Jake muttered, cursing the fates that had delivered Zeke to the grill tonight of all nights.

"All I said was—"

"I heard what you said."

"Well, excuse me for taking an interest in you, same as I always have."

Jake sighed heavily. "Sorry," he apologized and meant it. "There's no reason for me to take my foul temper out on you."

"Sara seems to be a little short-tempered these days, too. Any connection?"

Jake scowled at the far too perceptive old man. "Drop it, okay?"

"If you say so. Just thought you ought to know that it's hurting her concentration, which, as we all know, wasn't that great to start out with."

Alarm instantly flared deep in Jake's belly. His protective instincts kicked into high gear.

"She's fallen?" he asked.

Jake rolled his eyes heavenward. "Hell, boy, that's a given. Last time, though, she forgot to let go of the reins. Horse pretty near dragged her to hell and back. Scraped her up pretty good."

Jake was off the bar stool in a flash. "Take care of my check, will you? I'll pay you later."

"Where the devil are you going?"

Based on the satisfied gleam in Zeke's eyes, Jake had a feeling the question was merely cursory. "On second thought,'' he said, ''forget the payback. To-night's drinks are on you.''

Zeke nodded soberly. "Least I can do.''

Jake hesitated. "You know, old man, you are a pain in the butt. No offense.''

"None taken. It's the only way I know to get along with an ornery cuss like you.''

It was a familiar ritual. They could have gone on trading barbs for hours on end, but an image of a scraped and bleeding Sara plagued Jake too badly. He cut the conversation short and headed back to the ranch.

Fortunately, driving at a recklessly fast speed required all of his concentration. He thanked heaven he'd only had that one sip of beer so he was no danger to anyone as he sped home. Concentrating also kept him from wondering why his heart had plummeted when Zeke had delivered his news about Sara's accident. He might have been forced to admit that he really cared.

Up in her room, Sara was dabbing antiseptic cream on burning scrapes from head to toe when she heard the roar of an engine being pushed to the limits of its endurance.

Drawn to the window by the noise, she spotted Jake's truck careening up the driveway. He hit the brakes so hard it sent gravel spewing in every direction.

He was out of the truck before the motor died. He left the lights on and the front door sitting open. She gathered he was in a bit of a hurry, which definitely aroused her curiosity. Had the deal for the ranch gone sour? Could she be that lucky?

When the front door crashed open downstairs, Sara tiptoed into the hallway to see what all the commotion was about. Rather than heading straight for her father's office, Jake stopped squarely in the middle of the front hall.

To her astonishment, he stood right there and roared her name. When he spotted her, he took the stairs two at a time.

With her gaze fixed on Jake, Sara was only marginally aware that the door to her father's office had flown open and that he was staring after Jake.

"What the devil? Boy, have you gone and lost your mind?" he shouted after him.

Jake's gaze never left her face. His hands settled gently on her shoulders. "Are you okay?"

Stunned to silence by the fierce glitter of genuine concern in his eyes, Sara could only nod.

"Are you sure? Zeke said you fell and the horse dragged you."

Ah, she thought, so that was what this was about. Her latest debacle. Zeke had definitely been busy. She'd only limped away from his place an hour and a half earlier.

"I'm fine," she reassured him softly, casting a worried glance toward her father.

Jake followed the direction of her gaze, saw Trent and released her so suddenly she almost fell.

"Would somebody tell me what the devil is going on around here?" Trent demanded.

Sara glanced into Jake's eyes, pleading with him

silently not to tell her father what had happened. Since Jake had a vested interest in keeping their plans a secret, she was fairly certain she could count on him to improvise something to get them out of this awkward situation.

"One of the men just told me that Sara had taken a spill from her horse this afternoon," he said without missing a beat.

Sara supposed she ought to be grateful for his glib tongue, but she wondered how a woman could ever trust a word that came out of his mouth. She waited expectantly to see how far he carried this particular theme.

"From what the hand said, I thought it might have been worse than it apparently was. I figured I ought to come by and check on her," Jake concluded, which of course didn't explain why he'd been in such a frantic rush.

But it was close enough to the truth to satisfy her father without revealing anything damaging. Sara mouthed a silent, "Thank you."

Even so, her father climbed the stairs to join them, his expression worried. His sharp gaze surveyed her from head to toe.

"No damage done?" he asked. "You're sure?"

"Daddy, I've been falling off horses since I was little more than a baby. I'm pretty good at it by now," she said dryly.

He shook his head. "You always did have more gumption than sense," he agreed. "Never hesitated to get right back on. I kept thinking you'd wind up afraid of the creatures, but you never did."

He gave Jake a grateful glance. "Thanks for checking on my girl. You're a good man, Jake. One of these days you're going to find a woman who'll appreciate that kind of caring."

Color burned in Jake's cheeks. Sara had to avoid his gaze to keep from chuckling at his obvious discomfort.

"Maybe he already has," she said quietly.

Jake choked at that. Her father stared at him with sudden fascination. Sara had known exactly what she was doing by dropping that particular hint. Her father would never let it rest. He'd plague Jake about it until he squirmed.

"Is that so?" he said with satisfying predictability. He took Jake's arm and propelled him toward the stairs. "Let's go down to my study and you can tell me all about her."

Jake shot a dire look in Sara's direction as her father led him back down the stairs. She would have given just about anything to be an invisible speck on the wall in that room while her father cross-examined Jake about this new love of his. She had a feeling, though, that she would pay dearly for her part in provoking that conversation.

"Jake," she called after him.

He glanced back at her.

"You might want to go out to your truck and turn off the lights and shut the door," she suggested sweetly. "Otherwise, you'll have a dead battery by morning."

That reminder of his earlier rush would either add fodder to the conversation to come or give Jake the

excuse he needed to hightail it out of the house and
avoid Trent's curiosity all together.

The amused, knowing look she got for her trouble
told her he was fully aware of the lifeline she'd
thrown him.

"Thanks for reminding me." He gave his boss a
regretful look that was about as sincere as a snake
oil salesman's after a product failure. "Sorry. Another time, maybe. I'm beat and tomorrow's going
to be a busy day. Once I'm out there, I might as well
head on home."

"Whatever you say," Trent said agreeably, but he
was clearly disappointed.

Sara slipped hurriedly back into her room. Without
Jake to plague with his questions, her father might
very well decide to come upstairs and bug her for
answers. Pumping her for information would be far
more dangerous than taunting Jake. Sara wasn't
nearly as adept at hiding her feelings.

Just in case, she hopped into bed, pulled the covers
up snugly and switched off the light.

Sure enough, minutes later she heard her father's
heavy tread on the stairs. He paused outside her door,
then apparently reached the conclusion that she was
in bed, because he slowly walked on to his own
room.

Only when she heard his door shut did she breathe
a sigh of relief.

Unfortunately, it was a short night and her father
had a long memory. He was eagerly awaiting her
arrival the next morning when she went downstairs

for breakfast. He waited until she'd filled her plate
with eggs, sausage and toast and taken her first sip
of coffee before fixing her with a penetrating gaze.

"You really okay?"

She forced her brightest smile. "Fit as a fiddle."

"Jake seemed mighty concerned about you last
night. You sure that fall wasn't worse than you're
letting on to me? He's not the kind of man to make
a mountain out of a molehill."

"You can see for yourself that nothing's broken."
She was tempted to stand up and dance a jig to prove
it, but resisted the urge. Her father wouldn't appreciate the gesture.

"Where did it happen?"

They were wandering onto tricky turf, Sara
thought grimly. She dearly regretted being unable to
make a mad dash from the room. That really would
stir up a hornet's nest of unanswerable questions.

"A couple of miles up the creek," she improvised.
"It was slippery. The horse lost her footing and
stumbled. I wasn't paying attention."

"Woolgathering again," her father concluded.
"Sara Jane, how many times have I told you—"

She held up a hand. "More than enough."

"You don't seem to hear me. Maybe you should
stay off of horses."

He might as well tell her to stop breathing, Sara
thought angrily. Especially now when so much was
riding on her horsemanship skills. She held her temper in check and shook her head.

"It was nothing," she insisted.

If he knew what she was really up to, he'd probably go into cardiac arrest right before her eyes. "Stop being such a worrywart," she pleaded. "Nothing awful's happened to me yet. Just some bumps and bruises. I know for a fact you've suffered worse."

"Which just proves that there's always a first time," he said grimly.

"Enough, please. I'm a grown woman. It's my decision. I love to ride and I'm not about to stop."

He sighed. "Okay, okay." After a moment, his expression brightened. "So, what do you know about this woman in Jake's life?"

Sara almost choked on her scrambled eggs, before managing a reply. "Not a thing."

"But you said—"

"I was just speculating," she insisted. "Jake's an attractive man. He'd be a terrific catch. How could there not be a woman in his life?"

"Seems to me he's gone out of his way to avoid getting involved up until now," her father observed.

Sara grinned. "You were pretty fast on your feet, too, until Mama came along," she reminded him.

A nostalgic gleam lit her father's eyes. His expression softened. "Indeed. I suppose even the wildest soul can be tamed when the right woman comes along."

Struck by an unexpected insight, she asked, "You still miss her, don't you?"

Her father reached for her hand and squeezed. "Every minute of the day."

The sorrow in his voice was enough to soothe some of Sara's anger over his decision to sell Three-

Stars and flee to someplace with no memories. She could understand that kind of heartache. She had a feeling when things with Jake ended, as they almost inevitably would, her own heart would ache just as long and just as deeply.

Which made keeping her love for him a secret more important than ever. She wouldn't have everyone regarding her with pity or, worse, amusement that she had dared to think that a man like Jake Dawson could possibly fall in love with her.

Chapter Eleven

As the days passed without anyone discovering
what she was up to, Sara grew increasingly certain
that her secrets were safe. No one except Ashley
knew about her relationship with Jake, if that's what
it could be called. Only Mary Lou and Zeke knew
about their outrageous bet. With any luck at all they
would make it all the way to the end without inter-
ference from anyone in her overprotective family.

She prayed a dozen times a day that the secrecy
would last. Unfortunately, Riverton was a small
town. Sooner or later, she feared that someone would
get wind that she was sneaking off every day trying
to learn to stay on the back of a spitting-mean horse.

And when they did, there would be a lot of fas-
cinated questions. She doubted anyone would assume
that Trent Wilde's daughter had suddenly decided to

take up a rodeo life-style. Once gossip started, her father and Dani were bound to hear it and the meddling would begin.

Worse than worrying about discovery, though, was trying to stave off Jake's increasing attempts to talk her out of competing at all. Ever since her last fall when she'd stupidly gotten tangled up in the reins, he'd been more intent than ever on getting her to call it quits.

Perversely, each overly solicitous offer to end their challenge made her more determined than ever to see their bet through. At some point, it had gone beyond merely claiming the ranch. Her pride had kicked in. She wanted to impress Jake, at least in those rare moments when she wasn't inclined to throttle him for his suddenly overbearing protectiveness. He was rapidly getting to be worse than her father or her sister on that score.

If he started hovering over her at her lessons, she was going to have to kill him. She had told him as much just that morning. Her adamant declaration had kept him from coming with her to Zeke's, but in the rearview mirror, she'd seen that his worried gaze had followed her until she drove out of sight. A foolish woman might have assumed he really cared. She was more certain he was just worried about the burden of guilt he'd feel if something happened to her.

No doubted he'd maintained phone contact with Zeke all morning. Zeke had had his cell phone glued to his ear all during her lesson and he'd been mumbling into it the whole time, until even Mary Lou had grown impatient and told him to hang up or leave. Patches of color darkening his cheeks, Zeke had stuffed the phone in his pocket.

Even with all the distractions, Sara had managed to stay on the bronco for a full five seconds, her longest time ever. But with only a little over a week to go, that wasn't nearly long enough. Those last three seconds loomed impossibly before her.

When she finally dragged into the house at the end of the day, Annie poured her a tall glass of lemonade and set a plate of freshly baked gingersnaps in front of her. Her purposeful gaze indicated she wasn't gearing up for a few minutes of idle chitchat.

"Maybe it's time you told me what you've been up to," she said mildly.

Startled, Sara stared into the housekeeper's implacable face. "I don't know what you mean."

"Horsefeathers!" Annie said succinctly.

"Really," Sara insisted. "I have no idea what you're talking about."

"Maybe you can tell that to your father and he'll believe you, but that's because he doesn't look for trouble. I look at you and I look at Jake and I see trouble brewing with a capital *T*."

Sara tried to buy time by biting off a piece of gingersnap and chewing it very slowly. She sipped at her lemonade. When Annie's expression grew increasingly impatient, Sara sighed and tried to figure out an explanation that would satisfy Annie's curiosity without giving away the truth.

Before she could come up with a single half truth, Annie said, "I already knowing you're sleeping with him, so you could start with that."

Sara's mouth gaped. "How on earth did you know that?"

Annie gave a curt little nod of satisfaction at the blurted response. "Then it is true."

Sara's shoulders sagged. "You didn't really know anything, did you?"

"I was ninety-eight percent certain, but Jake denied it. You're not as good at skirting the truth as he is."

"Maybe those are the lessons I ought to be taking from him," she muttered under her breath.

"What was that?"

"Never mind."

Annie didn't pursue that, but she was hardly through with her inquisition. Sara could tell from the housekeeper's expression that she might as well settle back and prepare for a cross-examination that would rival anything ever done in a courtroom.

Annie had always considered the three Wilde girls her own. She'd bossed them around, bandaged their cuts, stuffed them with milk and cookies and surrounded them with her generous love. Her exuberant nature had been a stark contrast to their mother's more formal brand of nurturing.

She considered meddling her God-given right. No one in the household had ever dared to argue with her, not even their father. In fact, Sara had always wondered if Annie wasn't more suited to her father than her mother was, despite the very deep love the two had shared. Annie never hesitated to speak her mind, something the genteel, well-mannered Jessica Wilde had done rarely.

"I suppose this has something to do with your daddy selling the ranch to Jake?" she said now. "You figuring on keeping a place here by sleeping with the new owner?"

Thoroughly indignant at the unfair accusation, Sara opened her mouth to explain, but Annie held up her hand. "Not that I blame you for that. What your father is doing today is a crying shame."

Sara's heart plummeted. "Today?" she said weakly.

Guilt spread across Annie's face. "You didn't know?"

"Know what?"

"That they're in town at the bank right this minute closing the deal." Suddenly Annie's arms closed around her in a fierce hug. "Oh, baby, I'm sorry. I thought for sure you knew."

Tears spilled down Sara's cheeks. She brushed them away impatiently. "I knew it was coming," she said, half to herself. Her heart aching, she stared at the housekeeper. "I just didn't know that today was the day. Jake never said a word."

"And naturally your daddy didn't have the gumption to, either. I swear, that man has the sensitivity of a cactus."

The image made Sara smile, when little else could have.

"Maybe that's because deep down he knows how badly he's going to hurt me, hurt all of us."

"Or maybe it's just because he's an old fool," Annie said vehemently. "I should have given him a piece of my mind before things got this far along, but for some reason I thought..." She shook her head. "Well, never mind what I thought. It was just a foolish old woman's imagination, I suppose."

Sara was too upset to wonder what Annie had left unspoken. "I think I'll go up to my room now," she said dully. "I need to be alone." She shot a wry look at the housekeeper. "Of course, I suppose it's not even my room by now. I wonder when Jake will want me to go."

Annie gently brushed the tears from her cheeks. "Now that's one thing I know you don't have to worry about. He told me you'd always have a place here."

But unless it was as the owner of Three-Stars or as Jake's wife, Sara couldn't see how she could possibly consider staying on. The importance of the upcoming bronc-riding contest had just escalated.

Upstairs, feeling more lost and alone than she ever had before, Sara settled into a rocker and sat staring out the window, watching for her father or Jake to return. She wondered which one of them would actually tell her. Or would they maintain their silence on the subject until her father literally packed his bags and moved out sometime in the dark of night?

It seemed like hours before she finally spotted a swirl of dust in the distance. She watched as a car finally came into view, but it wasn't either her father's or Jake's. Instead, it was Dani's.

The minute her sister came upstairs, Sara realized that some part of the secret was out. The worried expression on Dani's face gave it away. The only question was just what her sister had discovered.

"You found out, didn't you?" she said bleakly.

"That you've lost your mind," Dani said with a curt nod. "Indeed I did. There I was in the general store a half hour ago, delivering my pies, when what do I hear but Mrs. Comstock and Mrs. Wingate gossiping to beat the band about you being over at Zeke Laramie's day in and day out taking bronc-riding lessons. Sara, what on earth are you thinking?"

"You don't know the half of it," Sara muttered, but Dani was on a roll and didn't hear her.

That inauspicious opening was followed by a litany of worries and frustrations, peppered with uncharacteristic expletives that had Sara's eyes widening.

"Of all the noodle-headed ideas you've ever had, this one takes the cake," she declared eventually.

Sara waited for more but that seemed to conclude the most long-winded tirade Dani had ever delivered to her younger sibling. She was pacing back and forth so fast, Sara was developing a crick in her neck from trying to follow her.

"Stop being so blasted independent," Dani added. "Stop trying to fight the world all by yourself, and let me help for once. Tell me what this is about. I know you didn't dream up this cockamamy idea for no good reason."

Tired of keeping everything bottled up inside, drained by the knowledge of what her father and Jake were up to at this very minute, Sara spilled everything. Her words tumbled out so fast that Dani clearly had difficulty keeping up. When Sara told her about Jake's insistence that she marry him if he won the contest, Dani regarded her with wide-eyed astonishment. Distress clouded her face.

"And you agreed to that?"

"Don't you see, it's a win-win situation," Sara argued.

"Win-win," her sister repeated incredulously. "How on earth do you figure that?"

"If I win, I get the ranch. If I lose, I still get the ranch."

"And that sneak, Jake Dawson," Dani reminded her ominously while still pacing.

"How bad can that be?" Sara asked staunchly, then added what was possibly the most massive understatement she'd ever uttered. "He's presentable, a little contrary maybe, but I can handle that."

"Given your own nature, I'm sure you can," her sister replied dryly. "Call me old-fashioned, but I thought marriage was supposed to be about love."

"It would be. I love this ranch."

"I was referring to Jake."

"We'll get used to each other." Actually, there was plenty of proof that that, too, was a massive understatement. She didn't think Dani was ready to hear that just yet.

"It's nice to hear you have such high expectations for the relationship." Dani paused smack in front of Sara and leaned down to stare straight in her eyes. "Have you bloody well lost your mind? You could be killed. What good will this stupid ranch do you then?"

Sara winced. Jake had told her the same thing a dozen different ways. Zeke had stopped voicing the same concern, but it was written all over his face every time she climbed onto a horse. Hearing it spelled out by her sensible older sister, who had no personal stake in the bet's outcome, made it seem more ominous.

"I won't be," she insisted firmly.

"You won't be," Dani echoed, then shook her head. "Your confidence isn't anywhere near as reassuring as you seem to think."

"I stayed on for five whole seconds today," Sara boasted. "Zeke says I'm getting better every day."

"Zeke Laramie has the brains of a mosquito. I wouldn't rely on his opinion."

"He was a bronc-riding champ when Jake was still in diapers."

"And he fell on his head a few too many times, if you ask me," Dani snapped. "The whole bunch of you have lost your minds. We'll see what Daddy has to say about all of this."

She whirled and marched toward the door, intent on blowing Sara's scheme out of the water.

Sara finally lost it. "Danielle Wilde, if you say one word about this to Daddy, I will never speak to you again," Sara declared, halting her sister in her tracks. To her surprise, when Dani turned back there were tears in her eyes.

"Sara, please. This is foolishness. Talk to Daddy yourself. Tell him what you're prepared to do to keep the ranch. If anyone's entitled to it, you are. I'll back you up. So will Ashley. We both know it's all you ever wanted in life.''

Maybe that could have worked once, if she hadn't been too proud to talk to her father when this whole mess started. Now, though, it was too late. Way too late.

''They're in town right now closing the deal,'' she admitted, trying to keep a thoroughly defeated note out of her voice. She crossed the room and hugged her sister tightly. ''Please, it will be okay. I know what I'm doing.''

Dani sighed. ''How soon will this so-called contest take place?''

Sara heard the resignation in her sister's voice and knew she'd won this battle, if not the war. ''Next week.''

''I wish you luck,'' Dani whispered, brushing at the tears dampening her cheeks. ''One last thing.''

''What?''

''Call the lawyer.''

''Why?''

''If I were you, I'd want to have all my affairs in order before getting within a hundred yards of that horse.''

Sara shuddered a little even as she silently conceded it was probably darn good advice.

Jake's hand shook as the president of the Riverton Bank pushed the final papers concluding the sale in front of him for his signature. Pen poised, he hesitated, thinking suddenly of Sara and what this moment meant to her. For him it was the beginning of everything he'd ever dreamed of. For her, it was a bitter ending.

"Don't go getting buyer's remorse at this late date," Trent Wilde said. "Sign those papers so we can get on with the celebration. You'll have your ranch and I'll be halfway to Arizona before sunup."

"Sneaking out in the dark of night?" Jake inquired with a surprising edge of sarcasm.

Trent didn't take offense. "That's my worry."

"It's mine, if you don't fill your daughters in before you go."

"Is that why your hand's shaking? You scared of my girls?"

"Only one," Jake said honestly.

"Sara, I suppose. I thought the two of you always got along. Certainly has looked that way lately. I know the two of you have been sneaking around behind my back."

Jake's startled gaze shot to his boss's face. Surely Trent didn't know about Jake's visit to Sara's room. A load of buckshot in his butt, not a casual remark, would be the more likely reaction to that knowledge.

"Sneaking around?" he repeated cautiously.

"I heard about the night the two of you went dancing at the Old West Grill. And I saw the way the two of you got along the night I had the Pattersons over. Put a damper on poor Harold's plans, I can tell you that."

"I have no idea what you mean," Jake insisted.

Trent glanced toward the banker, who was listening to the exchange with avid attention. "This doesn't leave this room, right, Logan?"

Logan Marshall looked thoroughly disappointed, but he nodded his agreement. Trent Wilde was not a man to cross, even if he was planning to leave Wyoming in the morning. Jake knew his influence in the state would last for years to come.

"You've always claimed you wanted no part of marriage, so I kept silent," Trent told him. "I had no right to meddle in your business. Now, though, I want you to know that if something were to spark up between you and Sara, I wouldn't object to it. She needs taming and I figure you're the only man on earth who might have a shot at accomplishing it."

"Selling me your ranch doesn't give you the right to plan who's going to move in with me," Jake pointed out irritably.

"Of course, it doesn't," Trent agreed a little too readily. "I'm just saying, if you want Sara, I'd give you my blessing."

Jake gave him a wry look. "I'm sure you know that Sara more than likely has her own ideas on the subject and very little of what you or I might want will influence her."

"That's the God's truth," Trent said adamantly. "They're all stubborn as mules, but she's the worst." He regarded Jake speculatively. "But something tells me the two of you might be a good match."

"Your matchmaking skills haven't been a resounding success up until now," Jake reminded him. "You picked Harold for her, for God's sake. If I were you, I'd stick to prowling around for a new dance partner for yourself and stop worrying about your daughters."

"Just putting my two cents in," Trent insisted. "Now sign those papers, son, before the ink in that pen dries up."

Feeling oddly bouyed by the unexpected man-to-man chat, Jake signed the papers. Even as Logan notarized them and gave him his copy, he had to keep repeating to himself that Three-Stars was finally his. He still couldn't quite believe it.

He hadn't dared to let himself dwell too long on this moment. Until just this second, when he'd tucked the signed papers in his pocket, he'd feared that something would go terribly wrong and all of his plans and dreams would go up in smoke.

Trent clapped him on the back and shook his hand. "Congratulations, son! I hope you'll be half as happy at Three-Stars as I've been. I know you'll turn it into the biggest, most modern cattle operation in the state."

Logan Marshall looked about as stunned as Jake felt. It was as if the banker couldn't quite believe that Jake had actually had the financial capacity to buy the ranching operation. Then he, too, held out his hand. There was a new measure of respect in his voice when he congratulated Jake.

"We'll look forward to doing business with you," he said with practiced sincerity.

Jake bit back a sharp retort about the amazing turnaround from the lack of welcome he'd gotten when he'd first walked through the bank's doors ten years before. Back then he'd been a scruffy, broken-down cowboy, with a small stash of money in his pocket and a dream in his heart. He supposed he could understand why no one then had taken him too seriously. Besides, it was time to put old insults behind him and move into the future.

He couldn't help wondering if Sara would be a part of that future, if he really wanted her to be. He tried to imagine Three-Stars without her strength and enthusiasm and commitment and came up blank. But then he wasn't sure he could imagine it without Trent Wilde bossing him around, either.

"I think a drink is in order," Trent declared magnanimously. "We'll have dinner at the Old West Grill. My treat."

Jake wanted to get back to the ranch. Back home. He had trouble even thinking of it in those terms. It was the very first place on earth that had ever felt like a real home to him and now it was officially his. Damn, but that felt good.

At some point during dinner, though, his satisfaction began to fade. He kept coming back to Sara and wondering what her reaction was going to be. She wouldn't be happy, no doubt about that.

Suddenly, he knew he had to be the one to tell her. He had to make her see that his fresh start didn't have to be her ending. Forget the certain outcome of the stupid contest looming before them, he had to persuade her that he wanted her at Three-Stars, by his side, sharing his vision of what the ranch could be. That was something they had always agreed on.

But in what capacity did he want her there, he asked himself over and over on the long drive back to the ranch? As a business partner? As a wife? Until he could answer that, did he have any right to intrude on the pain she must be feeling right now over the loss of her home?

Even though it was close to midnight, there was a light shining in her window when he drove up the long, curving driveway. Something deep inside him brightened at the sight. That light was like a beacon, welcoming him home.

Then reality intruded as he admitted that it only meant that Sara was awake and restless and probably fit to be tied. Unable to let the moment pass without some sort of peace offering, he walked over to the window, picked up a handful of small stones and tossed them lightly at the panes of glass. It only took three before the window flew up.

"What the dickens do you want?" she demanded, when she spotted him in the shadows.

Standing silhouetted against the light, her hair curling wildly to her shoulders, a robe clutched tightly to her chest, she took his breath away. He couldn't see her face, but there was no mistaking the fury in her voice. He watched her uneasily.

"I thought maybe we could talk," he ventured.

"It's late."

"But you're awake and so am I," he stated matter-of-factly. "And it's doubtful either one of us will get any rest until we settle this."

"I can't imagine what you're talking about."

Jake had no doubt that Sara knew by now about the closing. Annie surely would have told her, if no one else had. Though the deal had been kept secret up until the papers were signed, the veil of silence vanished almost immediately afterward. Word had spread through town by the time he and Trent had reached the Old West Grill. Someone would surely have spoken to Sara or Danielle by now, hoping for a reaction to pass along on the grapevine.

"Come down and I'll fill you in," he said, going along with her pretended ignorance. "I'll meet you in my office."

"Your old one or your new one?" she inquired sarcastically.

So much for the pretense, Jake thought. "The only one I have," he insisted.

He could practically feel her internal struggle. She didn't want to see him while her emotions were still so raw and yet she clearly felt she couldn't ignore his request.

"Give me five minutes," she said eventually.

"I'll make us a fresh pot of coffee."

"Planning on a long night?"

"We have a lot to discuss." He let it go at that and went on to the kitchen door. Inside, he fixed the coffee and carried the pot through the house to his office. He'd just poured himself a cup when Sara entered.

She'd changed into faded jeans and a cheerful green shirt, but she looked drained. Her eyes were dry, but a little too bright, as if she'd forced herself to hold back tears. Her lips were pinched. He wanted desperately to take her in his arms and tell her everything was going to be all right, but he didn't know that. Not for certain.

"I'm surprised you didn't chill one of Daddy's

best bottles of champagne for the occasion,'' she said, standing stiff and straight in the doorway.

"The coffee's more my style. Yours, too, as I recall."

She nodded reluctantly and accepted the cup he held out. When she'd taken it and perched awkwardly on the edge of the chair in front of his fireplace, he put his own coffee aside and hunkered down in front of her.

Once there, though, he was suddenly at a loss for words. Sympathy wouldn't be welcome, that's for sure. She'd find it hypocritical anyway.

"Nothing has to change," he swore to her solemnly.

Her eyes filled with a terrible, aching sorrow then. "Don't you see, Jake? It already has."

Chapter Twelve

Sara had promised herself that she wouldn't let Jake see how utterly defeated she felt, but the pitying look in his eyes just now told her she'd failed. She had never wanted him to feel sorry for her. She'd wanted to fight him fair and square, with every bit of ingenuity she possessed. She'd wanted to snatch Three-Stars from him in her own way.

But even though that was still a distant possibility, something inside her had died tonight while she'd awaited her father's return. She had never felt more lost, more at sea about who she was or her place in the universe.

Damn her father for doing this to her, she thought bitterly. He still hadn't had the courage to confront her. He'd slipped into the house just minutes before Jake's arrival. She'd heard him climb the steps, then pause outside her door. Her breath had caught in her throat as she'd anticipated him coming to her, admitting to her what he'd done, explaining his decision to her, maybe even apologizing to her for it.

The last was a laugh, of course. Trent Wilde saw no need to make excuses or apologies to anyone for his decisions, least of all his own family. He'd ruled Three-Stars like a benevolent dictator, generous at times, but asking no opinions and explaining nothing.

Her sweet, docile mother, who'd loved her husband to distraction, hadn't been bothered by his single-minded dominance. It had always driven Sara and her sisters crazy. Their constant struggle for a voice and, eventually, for independence had kept the household in a state of uproar that had thoroughly bemused their mother.

Tonight, even as she had waited with bated breath for her father to enter her room, she had heard him sigh and then move on. If he had struggled with his conscience at all, his conscience had clearly lost.

Given what she knew about his plans to take off for Arizona as soon as the deal was wrapped up, she wondered if she'd even see him in the morning or if he'd steal away before she awoke. She wondered if he felt any regrets at all, not over what he'd done to his daughters by selling off their heritage, but by walking away from his own.

She'd been about to rush down the hall and confront him, tell him face-to-face what a low-down, sneaky, conniving son of a gun he was, when Jake had appeared outside her window. All the heat and anger she'd churned up to take out on her father was now directed straight at the man hunkered down in front of her. She felt like slapping that sympathetic expression off his face, but she settled for sharp words instead.

"How does it feel to be a big, important man now? You must be feeling very smug," she accused.

"Believe me, sweetheart, smug is the very last thing I feel."

She deliberately ignored the compassionate note in his voice. "Don't try to convince me you feel anything like remorse, because I won't buy it. You wanted the ranch and to hell with anyone else who deserved it more."

He took the verbal slap without flinching. "An interesting choice of words," he noted. "Who gets to decide who deserves the ranch? Your father? He took what his father had built and turned it into a thriving operation five times as big. Are you suggesting he didn't have any right to decide what to do with it?"

"Legally?" she asked. "Of course, he did. Morally and ethically? That's a whole other ball game. Obviously neither of you understand those rules."

"Sniping at me won't change things," Jake replied. "At least with me as the new owner, you've got a chance to stake some sort of claim here."

Sara's response to that was a single expletive. Jake's eyebrows rose, but he kept on doggedly trying to make her see reason. She could have told him to save his breath, but it wouldn't have mattered. He clearly had some point he wanted to make.

"What if your father had made a better deal with

a total stranger?" he asked. "He could have, you know. He had offers over the years, some of them far more lucrative than what he and I had agreed to. You would have been out in the cold, if he'd taken one of those. Your bags would already be sitting on the front porch and the moving van would be in the driveway."

Sara stared at him, openmouthed. This was a new wrinkle she'd never anticipated. "He'd had other offers?"

"A half dozen that I know of," Jake confirmed. "One so sweet even I thought he was a fool for not accepting it."

"Then why did he sell to you?"

"For one thing because he's an honorable man. He'd made a commitment to me when I came here." He leveled a look straight into her eyes. "For another he knew that you and your sisters would always be welcome here as long as I owned it. He trusted me to make sure of that."

"How generous," she said bitterly. "Will you give us a discount on our room rates?"

An immediate and infuriating smile tugged at Jake's lips. "I'm not turning it into a bed-and-breakfast or a dude ranch, darlin'. And there are very few people I'd ever welcome here as guests." His expression sobered. "Even fewer I'd consider hiring on to work with me."

Shock spread across her face when she guessed his meaning. "You want me to work for you?" she asked incredulously.

"With me," he corrected.

"When you get right down to it, that's not much of a distinction."

"It is to me," he said.

He said it so softly that it made Sara's nerves tingle with sudden awareness.

"I know this is difficult for you," he said. "I know this is the last thing you expected your father to do, but it's done now. There's no going back. Let's figure out some way to make it work for both of us."

The sincerity and genuine compassion in his voice touched something very cold deep inside her, but it wasn't enough to take away the chill that came with knowing that this was no longer her home.

She had one last chance to change that and she intended to take it. She met Jake's gaze evenly, her shoulders stiff with determination.

"You're forgetting something," she reminded him. "In a week we're competing to see who will really keep Three-Stars. This conversation is premature."

Jake sighed heavily and stood up. "Right now you have a choice, Sara, one you can make of your own free will. How are you going to feel next week when you've lost and I'm holding all the cards?"

The prospect of that made her shudder, but she couldn't allow herself to think about the possibility of losing. "I'm going to win," she insisted. "How are you going to feel when I kick your butt out of here?"

He grinned at her defiance, a reaction she found both insulting and irritating.

"I am going to win, Jake Dawson," she insisted with pure bravado. "Just you wait and see."

Was she an absolute and utter idiot for not taking the deal Jake had offered her? Sara debated the question the rest of the night.

She was wide awake at dawn when she heard her father creep downstairs. Still dressed after her confrontation with Jake, she raced down after him. She caught him in the front hallway, a suitcase at his feet, a guilty expression on his face.

"Going somewhere, Daddy?" she inquired mildly. "Not without breakfast, I hope. You've always told us it's the most important meal of the day."

He regarded her warily, clearly uncertain what to make of her attitude. With obvious reluctance, he followed her into the dining room. Halfheartedly, he scooped up some fruit and poured himself a bowl of cereal, then sat down across from Sara. She waited patiently for the silence to start to weigh on him. It didn't take all that long.

"Go ahead," he said finally. "Get it off your chest. I can tell you're dying to tell me what a rat I am."

"Oh?" she said innocently. "Have you done something you're ashamed of?"

"You know damned well I sold the ranch to Jake. I'm sure Annie couldn't wait to break the news to you yesterday. She had enough to say to me on the subject when I got home."

"Apparently none of it registered."

"I did what I thought was best for all of us," her father insisted. "You included. There's money in the bank for each of you, enough so that you're free to do anything you want, though you obviously don't see it that way right now."

Sara fought to keep from bursting into tears. "Nope, I can't say that I do," she agreed. "But then you never cared much about my opinion, did you? Or Dani's? Or Ashley's? Who's going to break the news to them or were you planning to have your lawyer send them a clipping from the paper announcing the transaction? Or maybe the passbooks for their new savings accounts?"

He winced at that. "Okay, I deserved that. I suppose I just wasn't up to the three of you ganging up on me. I needed to get away and I knew if I admitted that, you'd all start fussing and hovering."

"Couldn't you have just taken a vacation?" she asked, unable to keep the plaintive note out of her voice.

"I needed to make a clean break. There are too many memories here for me." He sighed. "I'm lonely, Sara. And you know as well as I do that I'd never be able to bring another woman here after the life your mother and I shared. I need a fresh start and I'm fortunate enough to be able to make that happen."

As badly as it hurt, Sara forced herself to try to see things from his perspective. She'd never given a thought to why he wanted so badly to sell. How could she have been so blind to his pain? She saw him every single day. She should have known.

She reached for his hand. "I'm sorry. I should have realized."

"No," he said forcefully. "It's not your job to figure out what's going on in my head. Maybe I should have spelled it out, but I've never been much good at talking about how I feel. That's why your mama and I were so good together. She didn't need the words. She always knew what was in my heart."

"And you think you're going to find her replacement sitting around some swimming pool at a retirement center in Arizona?" Sara teased gently.

"Maybe not," he conceded. "But at least these old bones of mine will be warm."

"You're not old, Daddy."

"Maybe not in years, but since your mama died, my soul feels ancient."

"Then go on and find the fountain of youth," Sara told him.

Since there was no turning back anyway, there seemed little point in belaboring her hurt. She'd always been quick to anger, but just as quick to forgive. She was surprised to discover that the trait held, even for something as devastating as the sale of Three-Stars. Now that she understood what had motivated her father to sell, the betrayal didn't cut quite so deep.

"You'll be okay?" he asked worriedly.

Her lips curved briefly. "It's a little late to concern yourself with that now."

"You need anything, anything at all, you can go to Jake," he told her. "He'll always look out for you. I have his word on that."

If only he knew, Sara thought. Jake was far more of a danger to her than anything that might be lurking around the corner.

When her father drove off a half hour later, just as the sun was creeping over the horizon in a blaze of orange, Sara waved goodbye until he was out of sight.

The effort to be cheerful, to ease her father's guilt had cost her. Suddenly feeling all too alone and desolate, she couldn't bear the thought of going back into that huge, empty house...the home that no longer belonged to her.

She hurried to the barn, saddled up her favorite mare and rode out with no particular destination in mind. As usual, though, she was drawn to the ridge above the creek.

From that distant point she could look out across Wilde land and see the home she loved so dearly nestled in the stand of shade trees that were just now filling in with leaves. With snowcapped mountains in the distance, the view was stark and rugged, warmed only by that glowing sunrise that bathed it in golden light.

Tears filled her eyes and spilled down her cheeks unchecked as she forced herself to accept the possibility that in less than a week she would no longer have any claim to any of it. Not the house where she and her sisters had played and fought as children, not the barn where she'd saddled her first horse, or the creek where she'd learned to swim. None of it. It would all belong to Jake.

As if just thinking of him had conjured him up,

he rode up beside her. She felt his concerned glance, but she couldn't make herself meet his gaze.

With every fiber of her being she was aware of the precise instant when he slipped off his horse, tethered it to a tree and then returned to her side and held up his arms. Needing the comfort he silently offered more than she'd ever needed anything in her life, Sara dismounted straight into his embrace. She might hate herself later for turning to Jake, but for now the promise of his compassion called out to her. There was no mistaking the irony that Jake alone truly grasped what she was going through at this moment.

He tucked her head against his shoulder and looped his arms around her waist, surrounding her with his heat and his strength, but more importantly, with his tenderness and understanding. If she hadn't loved him before, she would have fallen deeply and desperately in love with him at that moment.

Because she needed his warmth and his compassion, she was able to suspend awareness that this was the man who'd stolen the ranch that meant everything to her. For just this instant, he was simply Jake, for so many years her reluctant best friend, her more willing mentor, and recently her very willing lover.

Silent tears turned to heartbroken sobs as she clung to him. He held her until she was spent, murmuring gentle nonsense that was so uncharacteristic of this sometimes harsh and cool-tempered man that it finally coaxed a smile from her.

When her sobs had quieted and smiling came more easily, she lifted her head. Jake's callused hands framed her face. His thumbs gently smoothed away the dampness on her cheeks as his gaze locked with hers.

"You sure you're finished now?" he asked.

She nodded.

"Good thing. I think the creek's about to rise to flood stage from all the tears you shed. I know my shirt will never be the same."

Sara tore her gaze from his and studied the soggy material. She covered mortification with daring. "Maybe you should take it off. It'll dry faster if you toss it over a bush in the sun."

She was suggesting much more and they both knew it. The sudden flare of desire in Jake's eyes was reassuring. With everything that had happened, that hadn't changed. He hungered for her in a way that stole her breath.

"Before breakfast, darlin'? I'm surprised at you," he teased.

"I've had breakfast," she told him archly and grinned. "Of course, if you're not up to it without some fuel in your stomach..."

He clasped her hand, drew it down and proved otherwise. She lifted her gaze to clash with his. With this man only did she dare such brazen things. She couldn't allow herself to wonder what would become of her if she never again met his equal.

"Then what are you waiting for?" she asked.

"I was thinking you might come to your senses. I can't be among your favorite people about now."

She touched a finger to his lips to silence the noble sentiment. On one level he was certainly right about that, but she needed his loving right now more than she needed to hate him, more than she needed to blame him for the unexpected twist her life had taken.

Because he seemed so determined to leave the final decision in her hands, she reached for the buttons of his shirt. She freed them one by one, ever so slowly, pausing to skim a fingertip across newly bared skin before moving on to the next button. Jake sucked in a sharp breath with each touch. His muscles clenched and rippled.

When Sara reached the snap on his jeans, she flicked that open as well, earning a soft moan for her trouble. His whole body tensed as her fingers dipped lower, teasing at the edges of the elastic band on his briefs.

"Sara?"

The soft whisper of her name barely broke her concentration on the smooth plane of his belly.

"Mmm?" she asked.

"When is it going to be my turn?" he asked in a choked voice.

The strain and tension made her smile. "Later," she promised. "I'm busy."

"Indeed you are," he agreed, amusement mingling with breathless torment.

Even as she taunted Jake with her increasingly insistent caresses, Sara could feel the heat swirling deep inside her. Without a single stroke of his hand, without a single deep and breath-stealing kiss, her breasts were achingly sensitive. Her blood thundered through her veins. Moistness pooled at the juncture of her thighs.

A sudden urgency ripped through her, escalating the game. She stepped back, startling Jake. With hands that shook she shoved down jeans and panties barely to her knees, then moved back against him, stripping away his pants and briefs just enough to bare his throbbing shaft.

"Now, Jake, please," she begged, her hands on his shoulders as she lifted herself to circle his waist with her legs.

His hands cupped her bottom at once to assist her. In a matter of seconds he was deep inside, filling her, moving with a slow, deliberate rhythm that was half the pace she would have set.

His satisfied, purely masculine smile told her he knew exactly what he was doing, knew exactly how sweet the torment was as he took her only so high, then waited an eternity before taking her higher yet.

When she could bear it no more, her hips moved instinctively to a more hectic rhythm that matched her quick gasps of pleasure and Jake's deeper cries of satisfaction.

The explosion of sensation, when it finally came, was more shattering than anything she had ever experienced. And if the thunderstruck expression on Jake's face was anything to judge by, he was equally shaken by the intensity of their climax.

The moment was both exhilarating and terrifying. Discovering that such a sensual crescendo was possible thrilled her beyond her wildest dreams. Discovering that only Jake could take her to such heights, however, suggested a subconscious level of trust that circumstances and logic told her couldn't possibly exist.

She told herself that that was what frightened her. How could her body be so completely, so thoroughly in tune with a man her head told her was destroying her world forever?

When she would have allowed that fear to come between them, when she would have fled in embarrassment and dismay, however, Jake prevented it. Still holding her, their bodies intimately connected, he lowered himself to the ground and settled her on top of him. His hands lingered on her bottom, smoothing over the curving flesh in light, persuasive strokes.

"Don't move," he whispered. "Stay with me like this for a while."

There was a faint, surprising note of desperation in his voice that Sara couldn't ignore.

"Why?" she asked, her breath fanning across his bare chest.

He was silent for so long she was certain he didn't intend to answer, but then he sighed.

"Because something tells me when you go this time, you won't come back."

Sara bit back a stunned gasp. That he could tell so much about her, that he understood her so well was as scary as the wild intensity of their sex. Only weeks or days ago, Sara had craved that kind of understanding, but now the timing and the man were all wrong. The fate of Three-Stars stood squarely and immovably between them.

That fate would be decided only days from now and it would be decided by an outrageous bet she had little chance of winning. But stubborn pride insisted that she follow it through to the bitter end.

Now it was her turn to sigh deeply as she studied the angle of the sun and realized that it was growing late. Her lesson with Mary Lou was scheduled for eight-thirty and she couldn't afford to miss even a minute of it.

"I have to go," she said, unable to keep the regret out of her voice.

"Where?"

"You know where."

"To Zeke's," he said dully. "Then despite what I offered you last night, you haven't given up on fighting me for all or nothing?"

Sara took one last, lingering look at the face of the man she'd loved practically forever, then slowly shook her head.

"You know I can't. Three-Stars means everything to me."

Maybe it was only wishful thinking, but it seemed to her that his eyes pleaded with her to say that he was more important, pleaded with her to stay.

But he had the same measure of stubborn pride than she did. He would never say the words, maybe couldn't even say what she desperately needed to hear—that he loved her. He simply released her and closed his eyes as she moved away.

Sara straightened her rumpled clothes and took one last, regretful look back as she went to her horse. Jake's eyes remained tightly closed.

Only when she had mounted and started away did he call after her. His voice was little more than a low-pitched whisper, but it carried on the breeze.

"Be careful, darlin'."

"I love you, Jake," she answered, but not aloud. The words were spoken only in her heart, where they could do no damage to her resolve.

Chapter Thirteen

By the time Sara got back to the house, all hell had broken loose. When she walked into the kitchen, Annie greeted her with a frantic expression.

"Dani's on her way over and Ashley's called five times," she told her. "They both wanted to speak with your father. When I told them he'd already left for Arizona, you never heard such wailing. Suffice it to say, your sisters are in a full-blown tizzy."

Sara groaned.

"It's too bad they didn't get wind of what he had in mind days ago," Annie added pointedly. "Maybe they could have stopped him."

Before Sara could respond to that, the phone rang.

"You get it," Annie said, backing out of the room. "It's probably Ashley calling for you again."

Indeed it was. Sara's greeting was barely out of her mouth before her younger sister started in.

"Has Daddy finally, flat out lost his mind?" she demanded.

It was apparently a rhetorical question because she didn't slow down long enough for Sara to respond.

"And you," she continued. "Why didn't you tell me about any of this? Dani says you've known for weeks now that he was planning to sell the ranch to Jake and take off on some crazy pilgrimage to reclaim his youth."

"It's not like that," Sara insisted, forced into the uncomfortable position suddenly of having to defend the indefensible. "Daddy just did what he's always done. He made a decision and he acted on it. He thinks we'll all be better off without Three-Stars to worry about. He's opened tidy little bank accounts for each of us to be sure we get our fair share. He says the money will give us the independence we've always craved."

"I don't give a damn about the money," Ashley insisted furiously. "Besides, that may be fine for me and Dani, but what about you? You love the ranch. I always thought you'd take over for him."

"So did I," Sara said softly, fighting back a fresh bout of tears. She deliberately drew in a deep breath before adding, "Look, I'll admit it threw me, but I have a plan."

"Spare me the details," Ashley said dryly. "Dani told me all about your plan. If you ask me, you're a couple of slices short of a full loaf, too. You can't possibly hope to beat Jake by riding a bronco. The man is in the Pro Rodeo Hall of Fame, for God's sakes."

"I am going to beat him," Sara retorted. "Which reminds me, I'm late for a lesson right now. Gotta go."

"Wait just one minute. I'm not finished. I'm coming home," Ashley announced determinedly.

That was all Sara needed, to have both of her sisters ganging up on her and trying to persuade her to call off the bet. "Don't," she pleaded. "There is no need to disrupt your life."

"I'm coming," Ashley repeated. "When's the contest?"

Resigned to the inevitability of her sister's decision, Sara sighed. "This weekend."

"I'll be there. Don't you dare get anywhere near that horse until I get home."

Sara tried one last time. "Ashley, you don't need to do this. You're too busy."

"Not at the moment," she said.

There was an odd note in her sister's voice that Sara couldn't interpret. She knew, though, that if Ashley had made up her mind to come home, there was no stopping her. She had her full share of the Wilde gene for contrariness.

And, judging from the hints Ashley had dropped lately, just maybe she needed to be at home for a bit. Maybe with a little prodding from Dani, a little of Annie's meddling and some of Sara's own brand of sleuthing, they could learn what was bothering Ashley.

"Okay, then, if that's what you want, come

home,'' Sara agreed with an exaggerated sigh of submission.

"I'd have been there before, if you'd told me sooner," Ashley chided. "We made a pact, remember? If there was ever trouble, we'd always be there for each other. I think this qualifies."

Sara smiled at the huge understatement. "You're right. I should have explained last time we talked."

"Well, never mind that now," her sister said. "I'm on my way as soon as we hang up. With any luck, I'll be there tonight. Love you."

"I love you, too. Can't wait to see you."

"Me, too," Ashley responded.

Only when the line had gone dead did Sara admit to herself how very glad she was that her sister had taken the decision out of her hands. No matter what the outcome on Saturday, it would be good to have both Dani and Ashley in her corner. She glanced up from the phone to see Dani in the doorway.

"Was that Ashley on the phone?"

Sara nodded. "She's on her way."

"Good. She sounded down about something and I don't think it was this mess with Daddy and the ranch."

"I thought I heard something in her voice, too," Sara agreed.

"Well, we'll know what that's about soon enough," Dani said briskly. "In the meantime, how are you?"

"Scared," Sara admitted. "With Daddy sneaking out of here at dawn, it's all so final. I guess I never thought it would really come to this."

"It's not too late to back out of that ridiculous contest. Maybe we could just go to Jake and make him an offer to buy him out."

"And what would we use for money?"

"I have some put away and I'm sure Ashley probably does, too. We could manage something."

"It wouldn't be enough," Sara said with certainty. "Owning Three-Stars means as much to Jake as it does to me. He's not going to sell it, not for any amount of money." She stood up and hugged her sister. "I've got to get out of here. I have a lesson and I'm already late."

A familiar worried frown puckered Dani's brow. "I really don't like this scheme of yours."

"So you've said, but I can't see that there's any other choice. Go bake some pies or something. It'll keep your mind off of all the things that can't be changed. By nightfall Ashley may be here and we can have a good, old-fashioned gabfest like we used to."

Dani sighed. "I suppose anything that can lure our jet-setting sister back home for a bit can't be all bad. Come by my house when you've finished your lesson, okay? I want to see for myself that you're in one piece."

"Okay, worrywart. See you later."

Annie, who'd deliberately given Sara privacy when the phone rang, turned up just then. Sara had the distinct impression she hadn't been far away. Her grim expression indicated she was aware of every word that had been spoken in her absence.

Sara left the housekeeper and Dani huddled together in the kitchen, probably plotting Jake's demise if she knew anything at all about their brand of loyalty. She'd have to remember to warn him...sooner or later.

When the bright red convertible came flying up the driveway spewing a trail of dust behind it, Jake knew at once that it was Ashley Wilde. It wasn't just that Annie had told him she was coming. He would have recognized that avenging-angel style of arrival anywhere.

Ashley had always been an enigma to him. With her cool, blond, ice queen beauty and her flirty smiles, she was a bundle of contradictions. One thing had always been perfectly clear, though. When it came to her sisters, she was very quick to jump to their defense. The only thing surprising about her arrival was that it had taken so long. She must have been kept in the dark about what was happening at the ranch up until now, he concluded.

Instead of heading straight for the house as he'd expected, she turned his way, an unmistakable, determined glint in her eyes. Jake braced himself for the kind of tongue-lashing only a firebrand like one of the Wilde sisters could deliver.

"You selfish jerk," she said without preamble, standing toe-to-toe with him.

He grinned at the deliberate crowding tactic. "It's good to see you, too. It's been a long time."

"That doesn't mean I don't know what you've been up to. How'd you do it? How did you persuade my father to sell you the ranch?"

Jake laughed at that. "You have been gone too long, Ashley. Nobody ever persuaded Trent Wilde to do anything he didn't want to do. He made a deal with me when I came here and he kept his side of the bargain. That's it. There was nothing devious or underhanded about it."

"How come none of us knew about this deal?" she asked suspiciously.

He shrugged. "You'd have to ask him about that. It certainly wasn't my place to run around broadcasting it."

"Oh, don't try to sound so blasted noble," she shot back. "You're enjoying all of this, aren't you?"

"I won't lie to you. I'm happy that Three-Stars is mine." He met her gaze evenly, his expression sober. "I'm not so happy about what it's doing to Sara. It's tearing her apart."

Blue eyes scanned his intently. Suddenly her expression softened. "That really matters to you, doesn't it?"

"Yes, it does."

"Then walk away from Three-Stars. Sell it to us or let her win that stupid contest. Just don't force her to leave."

"I'm not forcing her to do anything," Jake retorted. "I've given her choices. Maybe you should ask her about them."

Sara's car squealed to a halt just a few feet away before Ashley could respond to that. She took one last, searching look at him before turning to greet her sister.

Watching the two of them rush into each other's

embrace touched someplace deep inside Jake. As he
retreated inside, he wondered what it would have
been like to grow up with brothers or sisters, surrounded by love and taught the meaning of family
loyalty.

He also wondered what Ashley's arrival would
mean to his own plans to keep Three-Stars and persuade Sara to share it with him. With both Dani and
Ashley on hand to support her, would Sara dig in her
heels more adamantly than ever? Battling the pride
of one Wilde sister was tough enough, but all three
of them? He doubted he stood a chance.

Sighing heavily, he watched as Sara and Ashley
walked into the house, arm in arm, without so much
as a glance in his direction. He told himself he should
be glad that Sara had someone there to lean on. He
couldn't help hoping, though, that her days of turning
to him for comfort weren't over forever.

Now that the deadline was drawing close, he was
forced to face the fact that his life was no longer on
the uncomplicated, clear-cut path he'd planned for so
long. He cared about Sara. More than he'd ever
dreamed of caring for anyone.

But it seemed clearer than ever to him now that
no matter the proviso he'd tacked onto their bet, he
couldn't have both her and the ranch. He was going
to have to weigh his choices and decide which meant
more to him.

Sitting inside his cabin in the gathering darkness,
he thought about what he wanted and what was right.
It was long past midnight when he concluded that
his best choice would be to find some way to stop

that bronco-riding contest from ever taking place. Once it was over, no matter how it turned out, there would be no compromising or turning back.

Only one person he could think of was capable of calling a halt to it at this late date and that was Trent Wilde. He'd be so furious when he heard what was going on that Jake couldn't imagine him not high-tailing it straight back to Riverton and stopping Sara from climbing on that horse. He might find some way to get even with Jake for letting things go so far, but that was just a chance Jake would have to take.

He smoothed out the itinerary Trent had left with him. Though he'd allowed his daughters to believe he was leaving without looking back, he'd made sure that Jake could reach him in an emergency. Jake figured this qualified.

He dialed the phone number for the motel where Trent had planned to spend his first night on the road.

The operator had barely put through the call, when Trent grabbed the phone, sounding thoroughly alert. That ability to come awake in a heartbeat was a trait Jake had long admired in him. It had been honed through years of middle-of-the-night calls to deal with ranch crises.

"Jake, is that you?" Trent demanded.

His certainty about the identity of the caller proved what Jake had suspected. He'd given his itinerary to no one else, not even Annie. No doubt he'd feared she would only pass it on to his daughters.

"Sorry to call so late," Jake said.

"Is something wrong?"

"I suppose that depends on your point of view."

He took a deep breath, then described the bet he'd made weeks ago with Sara. "I couldn't see any way to say no to her. I swear I never thought she'd go through with it, but we're just a couple of days away from getting into that ring and she's as adamant as ever. The only thing I could think of to do was to fill you in. Maybe you can stop her."

"Oh, I'll stop her all right," Trent said fiercely. "And then, I'll break your damned neck."

"I was figuring on that, too," Jake said.

"I was so sure you could tame her," Trent said wearily.

"I don't think taming Sara is in the cards," Jake retorted. "And, frankly, I think any man who'd want to would be a fool."

"I see."

There was an amused note in Trent's voice that Jake didn't waste time questioning. "By the way," he told his former boss, "Ashley's here. They're circling the wagons."

Despite his obvious fury, Trent chuckled at that. "Maybe I won't need to break your neck, after all. With those three teamed up against you, you've got all the trouble you need."

"Don't forget Annie. My meals have been ice-cold and tasteless ever since we signed those papers at the bank." Pure mischief made him add, "I think maybe you ought to take her with you to Arizona when you head back that way. She seems to be missing your sorry hide."

"Forget about meddling in my life, son," Trent warned. "Besides, it seems to me like you've got enough to do to rescue your own hide from certain disaster.''

''You're probably right about that. I can expect you back tomorrow, then?''

''Let me give this some serious thought,'' he said. ''Sara won't be happy that you've drawn me into this. Have you considered that?''

''Oh, I'd say that's a dead-on certainty,'' Jake agreed. ''But she can be mad as hell at me, as long as she's safe. That's all that matters.''

''Jake?''

''Yes.''

''Maybe you should stop being a bloody fool and just tell the woman you love her. Seems to me as if that would solve everybody's problem once and for all. Marry her and Three-Stars would belong to the both of you.''

Jake swallowed hard as he absorbed the direct hit. ''What makes you think I love her?''

''A blind man could read the signals you're giving off,'' Trent said dryly. ''But if you're not ready to own up to it, I suppose there's nothing I can say to make you. Don't wait too long to tell her, though. You could lose her.''

Jake really didn't want to get into an analysis of his tumultuous emotions just then and especially not with Trent Wilde. ''Just get back here, okay?''

''I told you I'd think about it, didn't I?'' Trent grumbled. ''Give me a chance.''

''Don't think too long or you may not find your daughter in one piece.''

"You sure you're not just scared she's going to beat you and humiliate you?"

"Call Zeke Laramie," Jake suggested. "She's so bad he wanted to call off the lessons. She wouldn't let him."

"My God," Trent murmured.

"Prayers may help," Jake retorted. "But your presence would be better. The women of Arizona can wait a few more days." He paused, then added, "Trent, I wouldn't be asking, if I could think of any other way."

"I'll be on the road first thing in the morning," he promised finally.

Only when he had that commitment did Jake finally breathe a sigh of relief.

The moment didn't last, though. When Sara discovered what he'd done, there was most assuredly going to be hell to pay.

Chapter Fourteen

Jake had been so certain that his call to Trent would take care of everything. But when his former boss hadn't shown up the next day or the next, he'd grown increasingly frustrated.

How could Trent turn his back on everything that was going on in Riverton? Was he so irresponsible, after all, so uncaring that he was willing to let his daughter risk her neck? Was it going to be up to Jake to devise some way to force an end to the contest? He couldn't think of a single way to do it aside from just walking away and forfeiting his claim to the ranch. He doubted Sara would accept that kind of victory.

As the last minutes before the contest ticked by, Jake was torn between fury and panic. Ashley and Dani had gathered at Zeke's. The two of them were shooting daggers at him, even as they tried to bolster Sara's spirits.

To his amazement, Sara looked utterly calm and serene. Only once had she met his gaze directly. Her eyes were clouded with hurt, but her determined expression never wavered.

Jake couldn't believe that the whole thing had gotten to this point. A brilliant May sun was taking the lingering chill out of the spring afternoon, but his heart was icy with dread.

Without Trent's intervention, it was increasingly evident that he was going to have to either allow the contest to go forward or put a stop to it himself. Neither choice appealed to him. One way or the other Sara would be hurt, either physically or emotionally and he would be the cause of it. That would be the end of the bond between them and he'd grown increasingly reluctant to have that happen.

Watching Sara grimly preparing for this outlandish contest over the past weeks had increased his admiration for her tenfold. Even though he'd sneaked over to Zeke's more than once to watch her practice, he was facing the prospect of standing back and watching her climb onto that ill-tempered bronc today with a mix of respect and terror. How the hell was he supposed to live with himself if something went wrong?

He could tell himself from now until doomsday that this whole thing had been her idea, but he was the one who'd gone along with it. Anyone who was tempted to declare men the superior, smarter sex only had to look at him for proof otherwise. His brain had apparently turned to mush the second Sara had offered her ill-conceived challenge.

The smart, courageous thing to do would be to call the whole blasted thing off before she got her pretty little neck broken, but sometime in the past few weeks she'd gotten under his skin. He respected her for fighting so fiercely for what she wanted. No, if he were to be entirely truthful, it ran deeper than that. He was in love with her, whatever the dickens that meant.

At some point, he'd concluded that he wanted to win this contest in the worst way, not just to hang on to the ranch, but because he figured there was no way in hell he could convince a woman like Sara to marry him otherwise.

The crazy, impetuous idea of marrying her had begun to intrigue him the instant the spontaneous words were uttered. He'd been embellishing on it ever since, dreaming of just how hot and steamy and inventive sex would be with a woman of such deep and abiding passion. If she loved her ranch enough to risk her life to claim it, what would she give to the man who captured her heart? In her arms, he'd discovered that she was every bit as generous with her body as she was with her opinions.

During their long, lazy talks and frequent arguments, Jake had discovered that Sara touched his soul in some deep and elemental way that he'd never expected. Good sense told him it would never turn out the way it did in fairy tales. There could be no happily ever after for the two of them, but for the first time in his life he wanted to try.

That meant letting the contest go forward, giving her the chance she wanted so desperately to succeed, and then ultimately claiming her and the ranch as his prize. If he stopped it now, she would never accept his proposal. Even if she trusted his motives in asking, which he doubted, her pride would prevent her from saying yes.

"Who's up first?" Zeke Laramie inquired, forcing the issue.

"I am," Jake said at once, his decision made.

Perhaps if his own ride lasted long enough and was commanding enough, Sara could be persuaded to concede defeat without ever exiting the chute.

Zeke had talked an independent judge into driving over from Cheyenne for the contest, assuming there was any question at all about the winner. Perhaps his rating of Jake's ride would intimidate her. Judging from her contrary expression, however, it didn't seem likely.

"Whatever happened to ladies first?" she demanded.

Her belligerent tone amused him despite his gut-deep fear for her safety. "Afraid your nerves will take a beating watching me?" he countered.

"Not likely."

"Then indulge me," he said.

She looked him straight in the eye with that unblinking gaze he found both disconcerting and stirring. "I won't change my mind," she said softly.

Jake sighed. "Never thought you would," he lied.

His ride was picture-perfect, a replica of the demanding contest which had earned him his last championship title. The horse he'd drawn had been powerful, kicking with a ferocity that rattled his bones. Staying with him had been a challenge even to someone with his expert skills.

There was no doubt in his mind that the ride had been impressive enough to wither the hopes of many a true rodeo competitor. He could only pray it had been enough to dissuade a determined amateur like Sara, who had so much more than mere money at stake.

He glanced her way, but before he could assess his ride's effect on her nerves, a shotgun blast cut through the cheers of the handful of people who'd watched him perform. Heads swiveled in the direction of the sound.

Jake's gaze was fixed on Sara. He saw the color wash out of her complexion, watched as her shoulders unexpectedly sagged with defeat. Even before she uttered a word, he knew who had caused that reaction and it wasn't him.

"Daddy," she whispered in a choked voice.

Jake turned slowly to face Trent Wilde. Talk about cutting it close. The man's timing was off by days. Another few seconds and he'd have been too late.

"What the bloody hell is going on?" Trent demanded as if Jake hadn't already filled him in on every detail. He scowled first at Ashley, then at Dani, who was pale as a ghost, but who returned his glare unflinchingly. She slipped her arm reassuringly around Sara's waist.

"Ashley, darlin', I'm not surprised that you don't have the sense God gave a chicken," Trent said.

"New York'll do that to a person. But Danielle, I thought you had more sense than to let your sister do something this crazy."

Shoulders squared, Dani drew herself up to her full five foot eight. "Sara's a grown woman," she retorted, returning her father's gaze evenly. "Since you didn't give a thought to her when you made your deal, I think she has a right to fight for what she wants."

"Way to go, sis," Ashley chimed in. She scowled at her father. "I thought you'd be sunning yourself down in Arizona by now, spending all that money you got by selling off our heritage."

Trent winced at that. "I'd be there if I hadn't gotten wind of this craziness."

"Who told you?" Sara demanded.

Jake held his breath as he awaited Trent's answer.

"What does that matter?" Trent asked evasively. "I found out and I'm here to stop it before it goes any further."

He leveled a look straight at Sara that would have had a lesser person quaking in their boots. Sara didn't even bat an eye, which earned another measure of Jake's admiration, even as he rued her contrariness.

"Go on home, girl," Trent ordered, undaunted by Sara's expression. "A piece of land isn't worth your life. If you want a ranch so bad, I'll buy you one, something a little smaller and more manageable, something suitable for a lady."

Jake practically groaned aloud at Trent's ill-chosen words. He could tell from the fire in Sara's eyes that the sexist remark had merely fueled her already raging anger. She looked as if she wanted to explode, but she merely met her father's gaze with the same kind of serenity and conviction that had been shaking Jake to his core for weeks now.

"I don't want just any ranch," she declared flatly. "I want the one I grew up on, the one that belonged to my father and his father before him. Maybe you don't care about all that history, but I do."

In a last burst of defiance, her gaze clashed with Trent's. "I won't go, Daddy. There's too much at stake. I'm going to ride."

"Not damned likely!" her father bellowed. "Now get on home, girl." He turned his fury on Jake. "What the hell were you thinking of, Dawson? When I sold Three-Stars to you, I thought I could trust you to keep an eye on things."

"Things?" Sara repeated in an icy tone. "Am I one of those *things* he was supposed to be keeping an eye on?"

Trent ignored her outburst. His gaze never left Jake's face. "Well? What do you have to say for yourself?"

"Better men than I have had their brains addled by a pretty woman," Jake declared, his gaze catching Sara's and lingering until she blushed.

Trent was an observant man. He clearly caught the looks passing between Jake and his daughter and put his own spin on them.

"Well, hell, son, if you wanted to marry her, why didn't you just ask?" he inquired, causing a charged hush to fall over the small gathering. "I'd have given my consent."

Jake winced at the public pronouncement of the same notion Trent had expressed to him days earlier in private.

The blithe comment infuriated Sara as nothing else in Jake's memory ever had. Hands on hips, she stepped squarely in front of her father. The chill in her expression could have frozen beef. For once, Trent did look a little shaken by the tempest he'd stirred up, but he was not the kind of man to ever back down from a fight.

"Would you have thrown me in with the deal for the ranch?" Sara inquired bitterly. "Maybe given him a cut rate for taking me off your hands?"

"Now, Sara," Trent placated.

Jake noted that he appeared a little bemused by his daughter's increasing defiance, though he certainly should have been used to it by now. If so much weren't riding on this current battle of wills, Jake might have enjoyed the fireworks.

"Don't you dare take that condescending tone with me, Daddy," Sara commanded, poking a finger into her father's chest. "You've never taken any of us seriously. Not me. Not Ashley. Not Dani. We're your daughters and I'm sure you love us in your way, but we're disappointments to you because we're not the sons you wanted."

She waved off her father's shocked denial. "It's true. If you'd ever listened to me, really listened, you never would have offered to sell Jake the ranch in the first place. I know you wanted to get away, but you didn't need the money from selling the ranch to do that. You have more than enough salted away to live like a king for the rest of your life.''

Trent winced at that and opened his mouth, probably to offer some sort of excuse, but Sara didn't give him time to gather his thoughts. She had plenty more to say and Jake gathered she intended to get every bit of it off her chest.

''As for giving me some little, suitable ranch, do you have any idea how patronizing that is?'' she demanded. ''I know as much about ranching as you or Jake, but I've had to learn it the hard way, because you never saw fit to teach me a darned thing about what you always called *men's* work. You brushed off every serious question I ever asked.''

Tears shimmered in her eyes as she declared, ''Do you know how many credits I took in college on ranching? Enough for a second major. I've read every book in your library. I've plagued the ranch hands and the neighbors for lessons. There's not a chore at Three-Stars that I can't do as well as any man.'' She turned on Jake. ''That's true, isn't it? Tell him.''

Even as he nodded his agreement, Jake winced at the bitterness in her voice. She was practically quivering with rage and years of hurt.

He wanted desperately to go to her, to stand beside her the way a husband would have a right to, but he knew she wouldn't thank him for it. Dani and Ashley would have jumped to her defense just as quickly, but they too had apparently decided to let the scene play itself out. This was Sara's battle with her father and she had to see it through on her own.

In dragging Trent back here, Jake had set all of this emotional upheaval in motion and now he was helpless to stop the raw wounds being opened up.

"No more," she vowed.

She drew herself up. She wasn't as tall as Dani, but she was just as impressive in her determination.

"Back off, Daddy," she said as she brushed past him. "I have a bronco to ride."

Now there were two men watching with hearts in their throats as she climbed onto the horse and listened intently to Mary Lou's whispered, last minute instructions.

Jake warily eyed the horse she was about to ride, wishing he'd had a chance to test it for himself, wondering if Zeke had seen to it that she'd drawn one that would give her a flat, less dangerous ride.

Trent moved to stand beside Jake at the rail. Jake glanced over into his ashen face. "What the devil took you so long to get back here?" Jake asked.

"The damned car broke down in the middle of nowhere. It was two days before the blasted mechanic conceded he couldn't fix it. I had to buy a used pickup out from under some down-and-out cowboy to get back here at all." His worried gaze met Jake's. "Is she going to be all right?"

"I don't know," Jake said honestly. "Zeke and Mary Lou are the best instructors on the face of the earth. Sara knows the mechanics of what to do. The only question is whether she's got any natural talent at all." He studied the big bay horse again. "And just how mean-spirited that horse is."

With his eyes pinned on the chute, he waited, fists

clenched at his sides, his pulse hammering. Despite the eventual cost to himself, he found himself rooting for her to win. He'd find another ranch. He wondered, though, if he'd ever find a woman who was Sara's equal.

The gate opened and the outraged horse charged into the ring. The bronco wasn't nearly so concerned with Sara's dream. He pitched and bucked and shook her as if she were no more than a nuisance rag doll to be tossed carelessly aside at the first opportunity.

Jake was clinging to the railing of the ring with white-knuckled intensity, his gaze locked on that furious beast which held not only Jake's fate, but Sara's in the wild thrust of his powerful legs. The muscles in her arm strained as Sara held on for dear life and tried to keep her seat in the saddle.

Each critical second ticked by with excruciating slowness. Three. Four. Dear heaven, six. Two seconds short of the ride's necessary length. Her style might not be professional caliber, but her staying power seemed to be.

She could be a champ one day, he thought with a sudden burst of pride so fierce it took him by surprise. What she lacked in natural ability, she made up for with heart. Sheer determination was going to pull her through.

Just when he was exalting in her near-triumph, in a terrible sort of slow motion, she was in the air, tumbling toward the rock-hard ground, straight into the path of the horse's thundering hooves.

A half dozen men leapt over the rail in a split second, preventing disaster with heart-stopping inches to spare as they distracted the horse, then led him away.

Jake dived between the rails and reached Sara first. Oblivious to the bronco's fate and Trent's obscenities, oblivious to everything except the woman lying breathless and oh-so-still on the ground, he expertly and gently slid his hands over her. He checked fearfully for broken bones, shuddered at every scrape on delicate skin, waited with dread for those blue eyes to open and fill with tears of pain.

Instead, when her eyes snapped open, she searched his face anxiously. "Who won?" she demanded with the kind of single-minded concentration that made a champion.

Before he could reconsider, before he could curse himself for being a sentimental fool, Jake pushed his own dream aside.

"You did," he whispered, his thumb skimming along her cheek. "Three-Stars is yours."

He glanced slowly around at the stunned faces surrounding them, daring any of them to contradict him. When he was absolutely certain that none would, when he was sure that Sara was going to be just fine except for some cuts and bruises, he left her in Dani's capable hands.

And then he walked away without looking back.

Chapter Fifteen

Jake swore to himself that he'd be gone before Sara ever discovered the truth about what had happened in the ring that day. He knew that the secret wouldn't be kept forever. Someone was bound to blab that his heart had overcome his good sense.

It was too good a story, for one thing. The dedicated bachelor, the most commitment-phobic man in all of Wyoming, had fallen in love and given up everything. Romantics and cynics alike were going to have a field day.

He didn't want to be around to hear the guffaws of laughter. More importantly, he didn't want to be around when Sara got wind of what he'd done. Her integrity and sense of justice would force her to give up the ranch and the single noble gesture of his life would have been for nothing.

Whatever this thing was between them—love or something less mystical, such as unbridled passion, for example—it couldn't weather the kind of strain the fight to claim Three-Stars had created. Hell, his parents' marriage hadn't even been able to weather arguments over which brand of whiskey to buy. And that was the only example of so-called love he had firsthand experience with, unless he counted the rare, lasting passion he'd witnessed between Zeke and Mary Lou or the sweeter devotion between Trent and his wife.

He'd met privately with Trent that morning and arranged for the transfer of Three-Stars ownership back to the Wildes. He planned to take the money and move on, maybe to Montana, or even down to Texas, though he loathed the prospect of going back to the state where he'd been born. Maybe he'd just roam for a bit until he found a place that felt right, a place that felt like home.

Something in his gut told him, though, that without Sara, no place would ever again feel like home.

Well, that was just too bad. He'd lived on his own for years and he could do it again. One woman's touch was pretty much like another and he'd never had any difficulty finding women who wanted the no-strings kind of passion he was more comfortable giving.

Or so he told himself as he fought the gut-deep emptiness that had plagued him ever since he'd walked away from Zeke's the day before.

He saddled up his horse for one last ride over the

rugged terrain that had belonged to him all too briefly. In the morning, he would be on his way.

Though he set out to cover a wide expanse, he found himself heading straight for the ridge where he and Sara had made love. Sitting there, surrounded by so much raw beauty, memories crowded in and his heart ached for what might have been.

When he spotted the horse galloping his way, for just a moment his heart seemed to stop in his chest. Then he saw that the rider's hair was blonde, not red. Ashley, not Sara, he realized with something that felt an awful lot like disappointment.

She rode up beside him and sat for the longest time, silently absorbing the view. Then, a rueful expression on her face, she shook her head.

"I just don't see it," she said.

Jake regarded her with curiosity. "See what?"

"The same thing you and Sara do, when you look out at the land. To me it just looks like acres and acres of dirt."

Jake grinned despite himself. "You're a tough critic."

"At least you didn't offer up some cliché, like 'beauty is in the eye of the beholder.'"

"Isn't it, though? You see beauty in all that concrete in New York, don't you?"

"I did," she said in a way that sounded suspiciously as if she'd recently changed her mind.

"Trouble in paradise?" Jake asked.

Her answering smile struck him as forced, maybe a little too bright.

"I'm successful. I'm earning more money than I ever imagined. What could possibly be wrong?"

"I don't know. You tell me."

For an instant, he thought she might, but Ashley had always been more tight-lipped about her feelings than either of her sisters. She waved off his questions.

"I didn't come up here to talk about my life. I wanted to thank you. What you did for Sara yesterday was the most wonderful, heroic act imaginable."

He regarded her intently. "You didn't tell her what I did, did you?"

She held up her hands. "Not a chance. I got the message loud and clear. Besides, I've always been a sucker for romance."

"Romance?" Jake repeated, his tone deadly. He might know in his heart what he felt for Sara, but he would deny it with his dying breath. For good measure he added, "What the hell does romance have to do with it?"

Ashley didn't appear fooled by his attitude.

"You're in love with her," she said matter-of-factly. "You gave her the one thing on earth she wanted. I think that's sweet. A grand, romantic gesture."

Sweet? Heroic? Where did women come up with this stuff, Jake wondered. He'd done the only thing he could do under the circumstances. He told Ashley exactly that.

"The ranch should have been hers in the first place," he concluded.

"Well, of course it should," Ashley said. "That's

beside the point. When are you going to admit you love her?''

Jake's insides quaked at the thought of making such an admission, at the prospect of making himself so vulnerable to another human being.

"I'm leaving in the morning," he said flatly. "Does that answer your question?"

"No, that tells me you're a fool."

"Not a hero anymore?" he inquired dryly.

"Jake, I know a little about your past." She glowered at him. "Oh, don't get that betrayed look on your face. It wasn't Sara who told me. I just heard bits and pieces when you first came. At any rate, I know you don't believe in love. I'm not sure I do either, for that matter."

Her expression turned suddenly wistful, but she shook it off and went on.

"The truth is, though, when you look at Sara, there's a light in your eyes that looks an awful lot like the love I used to see shining in Daddy's eyes when he looked at my mother. It's in Sara's eyes when she looks at you. How can you walk away from that?"

He sighed heavily. "How can I not? She'll never trust my motives, if I stay. She'll always wonder if I'm saying I care about her, just so I can keep the ranch."

"Oh, for heaven's sake, it's just a bunch of dirt," she declared vehemently. "Stop letting it get in the way of the only thing that really matters, how you feel about each other."

"For someone who claims not to believe in love,

you use a lot of pretty words to describe it," he said, then deliberately dismissed her. "Thanks for coming back here when Sara needed you. Will you be staying?"

"Only if there's going to be a wedding," she declared flatly, fixing him with a challenging look.

"Then I suppose you ought to be getting on back to the house so you can book your flight."

Ashley scowled at the response. "Men!" she said scathingly. "You **are** the densest critters God ever put on earth."

Jake hid a smile. "You may be right about that, darlin'. You may be right."

He figured he'd have a lot of lonely years ahead to contemplate the truth of her assessment.

It was several miserable, lonely days before Sara was finally allowed out of bed again. People had been tiptoeing in and out of her room and talking in whispers until she was certain she would scream if it didn't stop.

"Enough," she finally declared and swung her bruised and aching legs over the side of the bed. "I'm getting up."

Dani jumped up and rushed to her side. Her hand, firmly placed on Sara's shoulder, held her down.

"Maybe you should wait until the doctor comes," she said.

"I didn't break anything," Sara argued. "I didn't damage any internal organs. You said so yourself. If I stay in this bed one minute longer, my muscles will probably start to atrophy." She scowled at her sister.

"And why has everybody been whispering? Even Daddy's stopped blustering. Every time I look up he and Annie are huddled in the corner. What's the big secret?"

"No secret," Dani assured her, but her guilty expression said otherwise.

"Danielle Wilde, you never could lie worth two hoots. What's going on? Does it have something to do with Jake?"

"Why would you ask that?" her sister inquired blandly.

"Because unless I'm dying, I can't think of anything else you'd all be keeping so quiet about. What exactly happened on Saturday?"

"You were there. You know what happened."

"I fell, remember? I was knocked unconscious. What did I miss?"

Suddenly, she had a terrible thought. She'd been only vaguely aware of the time that had passed as she'd fought to stay on the back of that miserable bronco. When Jake had told her she'd won, she'd assumed she'd managed to last the full eight seconds before being thrown.

"I lost, didn't I?" she said with absolute certainty. If her brain hadn't been so addled by that fall, she'd have known it right off. He'd had a perfect, championship-level ride. She'd seen every incredible, spectacular second of it herself.

Dani's sigh was answer enough.

"Oh, my God," she whispered. "Why did Jake tell me I'd won?"

Dani smiled. "I don't know for sure, of course.

But if I had to hazard a guess, I'd say it was because he loves you.''

Dani's guess should have thrilled her, but it didn't. Her heart sank. If Jake had made such a wonderful, foolish, grand gesture then he was all but declaring it was over between them. She dimly recalled the sad expression on his face as he had walked away that day. Giving her the ranch had been his way of saying goodbye.

Over the next few days, as she struggled to come to grips with what she'd learned, depression settled in. She had what she wanted. Three-Stars was finally hers. It should have been enough. Surely she couldn't have hoped to lose just so Jake would be part of her future along with the ranch. And if she was missing him now, how deep would the hurt run weeks from now? Years from now?

At first when he didn't stop by for a visit, she worried that her father had stepped in and fired him on her behalf. Now she knew better.

"He's gone, isn't he?"

"Since two days after the contest," Dani admitted. "He signed over Three-Stars and left. No one has heard from him since, not even Annie. She's fit to be tied. She loved him as if he were a son. She's furious with Daddy, too. She blames him for setting all of this in motion in the first place. You should hear her slamming things around in the kitchen. It may be quiet up here, but it's anything but down there."

Sara felt as if the breath had been stolen straight out of her.

"Jake is really gone?" she whispered, staring at Dani with dismay.

"He told Ashley it was for the best. She tried to get through to him, she really did, but he's as stubborn as all three of us combined. I'm sorry, sweetie."

Sara refused to accept the fact that it was over. Once she was on her feet, she began making it her business to track Jake down. She went about it with the same grim determination with which she'd tackled learning to ride that stupid bronco.

Jake was enough of a celebrity that he was bound to be spotted fairly easily anywhere in rodeo country. It shouldn't take more than a few days to pick up his trail.

She hired a private detective to be sure that the discovery of that trail came sooner, rather than later. She couldn't risk having Jake push whatever he felt for her into some cold, dark place deep inside him where he could shut it away and pretend it didn't exist.

"Damn, you're jumpier than a flea," her father declared after observing her silently across the breakfast table for the third morning in a row. His expression sobered. "You really do love him, don't you?"

Sara saw no point in trying to hide it. "I think I've loved him since the first day he rode onto our land," she admitted. She lifted her chin defiantly. "I'm not going to give up on him without a fight."

Her father smiled at that. "Did you hear me asking you to? If you fight for him as hard as you fought for the ranch, he doesn't stand a chance."

He paused for a minute, then added, "It's not go-

ing to be easy getting him to admit his feelings for
you. I tried to do it and couldn't get through to him."

To Sara's amusement, he sounded thoroughly
peeved about his failure to make any headway with
his matchmaking.

"Jake's developed a tough hide to protect himself
from hurt," he concluded. "He'll fight you."

"You don't have to tell me that," Sara said, then
added with grim determination, "But he's never
come up against a woman who loves him as much
as I do."

It took one long, endless week for the private detective to trace Jake to a small town in Montana.
"He's negotiating for a ranch outside of town," the
man told Sara. "The owner's anxious to sell and Jake
is offering cash, so it shouldn't take long for the deal
to go through."

And once it did, it would be all but over, Sara
realized. He would have his own land.

If he was paying cash, it couldn't be the spread
Three-Stars was, but maybe that didn't matter to him
anymore. Maybe he was ready to settle for second
best. She couldn't let him do that. Maybe it was time
to issue another dare.

She found Jake after two days of hard driving to
the northwest corner of Montana, so close to Canada
she wasn't entirely sure she hadn't crossed the bor-
der. Though the sky was a brilliant summer blue,
there were still patches of snow on the ground. She
shivered just looking at it.

According to the detective who'd waited for her
arrival, she was too late to stop the deal for the ranch.

The owner had turned over the keys to the place that morning. Jake was already out there.

She found him all alone, chopping wood, his bare shoulders glistening with sweat from the blaze of sun that fought the late spring chill. Filled with relief, she nearly wept just at the sight of him. Her heart skipped a beat, and then another.

At the sound of her car's approach, he glanced up and regarded her warily. Amazingly enough, he didn't seem all that surprised to see her. His expression didn't change as she walked over to him.

"What's up?" he asked as if they'd parted only yesterday.

The casual question didn't fool her. He was as tense as if he'd just spotted a rattler.

"I've been looking for you." She gestured around at the small, but tidy house and nearby barn. "You move fast."

"No point in delaying the inevitable. You find something that's right for you, you grab it."

"Is that so?" She fixed an even, considering gaze on him. "Am I the exception, then?"

The muscle working in his jaw told her she'd hit a nerve. Somehow, though, he managed to keep his expression perfectly bland.

"I'm not sure I know what you mean," he claimed.

"Then maybe we should back up a step. Start at the beginning, so to speak. I heard something from my sister a few days ago. I was wondering if it's true."

"You ever known your sister to lie?"

"No. But I'd never known you to lie, either. That's why I'm asking you straight out. Who won that bronc-riding contest, Jake?"

"You did, fair and square," he insisted.

Sara noticed he didn't look her in the eye when he said it. She nodded. "That's what I thought."

He appeared a little smug at having put one over on her. She killed that notion right off by adding, "Dani was telling the truth."

He swallowed hard at the flat statement, but that was the only reaction she got from him. She stepped closer until he was forced to meet her gaze. "You, on the other hand, are a bald-faced liar, Jake Dawson."

He blinked hard at the cool accusation. "A man would get shot for calling a cowboy a liar without cause."

"You want to talk about proof? Fine. Does the difference between eight perfect seconds and six sloppy ones ring any bells? My brain might have been addled by that fall, but sooner or later I was bound to catch on."

He sighed heavily. She took that as an admission. "Why, Jake? Were you so repulsed by the idea of marrying me that you were willing to give me the ranch just to get out of the deal we'd made?"

His expression darkened. Before she realized what he intended, he'd hauled her into his arms and kissed her with such savage intensity that her head was spinning. Every muscle in his body tensed as his mouth plundered hers. That pretty much answered any questions she had about whether he'd developed a sudden aversion to her.

"Oh, my," she whispered, when she could speak at all. Weak-kneed, she clung to him.

"Don't ever get it into that fool head of yours that I don't want you," he said fiercely.

"Then why?"

"Because it would be a mistake, that's why. You and I are nothing alike. I'm not marriage material. You're classy. I'm a broken-down ex–rodeo champ." He regarded her with obvious regret written all over his face. "Shall I go on?"

"I'm afraid you're going to have to," Sara said. "So far I haven't heard anything to justify your welshing on our bet."

"Dammit, Sara, it just wouldn't work."

"Because your folks had a lousy marriage?"

"That and because you deserve better," he insisted.

"Whatever happened to being partners? If I'm good enough to be your partner, then surely there's enough trust and liking between us to make a marriage work."

"It's not the same," he said stubbornly.

Sara shook her head. She thought she'd taken the biggest risk of her life a few weeks earlier, but apparently the real test was still in front of her.

"The way I figure it," she began in a soft, deceptively lazy voice, "you owe me one. And if lying is cause for taking a shotgun to a cowboy, then cheating is just as bad. Am I right? Code of the West and all that."

Jake eyed her warily. "I suppose."

"Well, it seems to me you've cheated me out of a wedding ring." She reached into her car and retrieved the shotgun she'd brought along for just this moment. She'd loaded it with blanks just in case she had to fire it to prove a point.

Jake's mouth dropped open. "Sara," he began, backing up a step.

"You ever heard the expression *shotgun wedding?*" she inquired, her finger settling comfortably against the trigger. She wouldn't hesitate to fire it if she had to and both of them knew it, though Jake still seemed to be in a state of denial.

"You wouldn't dare," he said.

She grinned. "Jake, you of all people should know just how daring I am."

"But why?"

"Because the minute I realized what you were willing to sacrifice for me, I had to admit that I was in love with you, flat-out, head over heels in love. I don't intend to let you and my ranch get away."

"I gave you the ranch," he reminded her, though a grin was beginning to work at the corners of his mouth.

"I'm greedy," she declared. "I want your heart, too."

He shook his head as if he couldn't quite believe this latest turn of events. "Well, I'll be damned."

"If you don't carry me inside and make love to me, you surely will be," she agreed.

And so he did.

A long time later, Jake was lying beside the sexiest, most passionate woman he'd ever known wondering about the subject of risks.

He'd taken a chance when he'd run off at fifteen with no skills and fewer prospects.

He'd taken an even bigger risk the first time he'd climbed on a bull's back.

And he'd thrown caution to the wind when he'd offered a challenge to the sassy, daring woman in bed beside him. He glanced down at her and smiled.

No doubt about it, he had well and truly met his match. Sara could put her shotgun away. They'd have to hog-tie him and throw him in jail to keep him from getting to the church on time.

Sara squirmed against him, setting his senses on fire. When he glanced down, he noticed that her eyes were open and there was a satisfied smile on her lips.

"I was just wondering," he said, his hand curving possessively over her breast. "How do you feel about long engagements?"

"Hate 'em," she said at once.

Jake grinned. "Good."

"Of course, we do have one major detail to work out."

"What's that?"

"We seem to be overburdened with property." She glanced curiously around the small bedroom. "I like this. It's homey."

Jake's hand stilled against heated flesh. "What are you saying?"

Her expression turned thoughtful. "We could stay

here. There would be fewer complications. It would
be a fresh start.''

He studied her face intently, trying to read what
was going on in that complicated head of hers. ''You
wouldn't mind?''

''Something tells me we might end up tussling
over whether Three-Stars was mine or yours. This
place would be ours.''

''We'd be starting from scratch,'' Jake reminded
her.

She shrugged. ''I don't mind hard work.'' She
stroked a finger down the center of his chest. ''I'm
especially fond of the fringe benefits.''

Jake pondered this latest turn of events. Staying
here would be an answer. It would prevent Three-
Stars from ever coming between them and yet...

''No,'' he said. ''I can't let you do it. Three-Stars
is your home. You fought for it. I love it as much as
you do. We'll make it ours.''

Sara scooted onto her knees and gazed down at
him. ''You're sure?''

''Darlin', when you're around the only thing I
know for sure is how badly I want you, but yes, I
think we belong at Three-Stars.''

She straddled his hips. ''I don't know, Jake. I'm
growing rather fond of this bed.''

''Then I suppose we'd better make use of it,'' he
said agreeably. ''It seems like the perfect spot for a
honeymoon.''

''And for romantic getaways when all the kids are
driving us to distraction?''

Jake stilled. ''Kids?''

"Of course," she said blithely.

Vaguely intrigued by an idea he'd always dismissed right along with the possibility of marriage, Jake stared at her in mock horror. "This is a new wrinkle. I thought Dani was the maternal one in the family."

Sara leaned down and brushed a kiss across his lips, then whispered, "You don't think I'm going to let those perfect genes of yours go to waste, do you? Auntie Dani can baby-sit every time we want to sneak up here and make another baby."

"And you see this happening often?"

"Oh, yes," she breathed as she lifted her hips and then slowly sheathed him deep inside her. "Very often."

A new sensation spread through Jake as they came together in an explosion of passion. It went beyond desire, beyond the fire of fulfillment. In fact, if he'd had to hazard a guess, it felt an awful lot like hope.

* * * * *

Watch for ASHLEY'S REBEL, coming in March 1997 from Silhouette Special Edition.

1

Morgan Brigham slowly set down his coffee cup on the kitchen table and stared at the comic strip in the center of his paper. It was nestled in among approximately twenty others that were spread out across two pages. But this was the only one he made a point of reading faithfully each morning at breakfast.

This was the only one that mirrored *her* life.

He read each panel twice, as if he couldn't trust his own eyes. But he could. It was there, in black and white.

Morgan folded the paper slowly, thoughtfully, his mind not on his task. So Traci was getting engaged.

The realization gnawed at the lining of his stomach. He hadn't a clue as to why.

He had even less of a clue why he did what he did next.

Abandoning his coffee, now cool, and the newspaper, and ignoring the fact that this was going to make him late for the office, Morgan went to get a sheet of stationery from the den.

He didn't have much time.

* * *

Traci Richardson stared at the last frame she had just drawn. Debating, she glanced at the creature sprawled out on the kitchen floor.

"What do you think, Jeremiah? Too blunt?"

The dog, part bloodhound, part mutt, idly looked up from his rawhide bone at the sound of his name. Jeremiah gave her a look she felt free to interpret as ambivalent.

"Fine help you are. What if Daniel actually reads this and puts two and two together?"

Not that there was all that much chance that the man who had proposed to her, the very prosperous and busy Dr. Daniel Thane, would actually see the comic strip she drew for a living. Not unless the strip was taped to a bicuspid he was examining. Lately Daniel had gotten so busy he'd stopped reading anything but the morning headlines of the *Times*.

Still, you never knew. "I don't want to hurt his feelings," Traci continued, using Jeremiah as a sounding board. "It's just that Traci is overwhelmed by Donald's proposal and, see, she thinks the ring is going to swallow her up." To prove her point, Traci held up the drawing for the dog to view.

This time, he didn't even bother to lift his head.

Traci stared moodily at the small velvet box on the kitchen counter. It had sat there since Daniel had asked her to marry him last Sunday. Even if Daniel never read her comic strip, he was going to suspect something eventually. The very fact that she hadn't grabbed the ring from his hand and slid it onto her finger should have told him that she had doubts about their union.

Traci sighed. Daniel was a catch by any definition. So what was her problem? She kept waiting to be struck by that sunny ray of happiness. Daniel said he wanted to take care of her, to fulfill her every wish. And he was even willing to let her think about it before she gave him her answer.

Guilt nibbled at her. She should be dancing up and down, not wavering like a weather vane in a gale.

Pronouncing the strip completed, she scribbled her signature in the corner of the last frame and then sighed. Another week's work put to bed. She glanced at the pile of mail on the counter. She'd been bringing it in steadily from the mailbox since Monday, but the stack had gotten no farther than her kitchen. Sorting letters seemed the least heinous of all the annoying chores that faced her.

Traci paused as she noted a long envelope. Morgan Brigham. Why would Morgan be writing to her?

Curious, she tore open the envelope and quickly scanned the short note inside.

Dear Traci,
I'm putting the summerhouse up for sale. Thought you might want to come up and see it one more time before it goes up on the block. Or make a bid for it yourself. If memory serves, you once said you wanted to buy it. Either way, let me know. My number's on the card.

Take care,
Morgan

P.S. Got a kick out of *Traci on the Spot* this week.

Traci folded the letter. He read her strip. She hadn't known that. A feeling of pride silently coaxed a smile to her lips. After a beat, though, the rest of his note seeped into her consciousness. He was selling the house.

The summerhouse. A faded white building with brick trim. Suddenly, memories flooded her mind. Long, lazy afternoons that felt as if they would never end.

Morgan.

She looked at the far wall in the family room. There was a large framed photograph of her and Morgan standing before the summerhouse. Traci and Morgan. Morgan and Traci. Back then, it seemed their lives had been permanently intertwined. A bittersweet feeling of loss passed over her.

Traci quickly pulled the telephone over to her on the counter and tapped out the number on the keypad.

*   *   *   *   *

Look for TRACI ON THE SPOT
by Marie Ferrarella, coming to
Silhouette YOURS TRULY
in March 1997.

Silhouette®

SPECIAL EDITION™

COMING NEXT MONTH

#1087 ASHLEY'S REBEL—Sherryl Woods
The Bridal Path
That Special Woman!
Forbidden passions sparked to life when ex-model Ashley Wilde
reluctantly shared very close quarters with handsome rebel Dillon Ford.
Can their turbulent past together allow them a passionate tomorrow?

#1088 WAITING FOR NICK—Nora Roberts
Those Wild Ukrainians
Here is the story readers have been begging for! To Frederica Kimball,
it seemed she'd spent her entire childhood waiting for Nick. Now she's
all grown up—and the waiting is over!

#1089 THE WRONG MAN...THE RIGHT TIME—Carole Halston
It was love at first sight when virginal Pat Tyler encountered ruggedly
handsome Clint Adams. But the ex-marine gallantly pushed the
beguiling young woman away. He thought he was the wrong man for
her. Could she convince him he was Mr. Right?

#1090 A HERO'S CHILD—Diana Whitney
Parenthood
Hank Flynn died a hero—or so everyone thought. Now he was back to
claim his fiancée—and the daughter he never knew he had....

#1091 MARRY ME IN AMARILLO—Celeste Hamilton
Gray Nolan would do anything to stop his baby sister's wedding—
even seduce bridal consultant Kathryn Seeger to his side. But this
commitment-shy cowboy quickly learned that Kathryn had no intention
of changing his sister's mind about marriage, and every intention of
changing his....

#1092 SEPARATED SISTERS—Kaitlyn Gorton
Single mom Ariadne Palmer just discovered she has a missing twin
sister! Placing her trust in the mysterious man who brought her this
compelling news, she must learn what family *really* means....

*If you're looking for irresistible
heroes, the search is over....*

Joan Elliott Pickart's

Tux, Bram and Blue Bishop and their pal,
Gibson McKinley, are four unforgettable men...on a
wife hunt. Discover the women who steal their
Texas-size hearts in this enchanting four-book series,
which alternates between Silhouette Desire
and Special Edition:

In February 1997, fall in love with Tux, Desire's
Man of the Month, in **TEXAS MOON,** #1051.

In May 1997, Blue meets his match in **TEXAS DAWN,**
Special Edition #1100.

In August 1997, don't miss Bram's romance in
TEXAS GLORY—coming to you from Desire.

And in December 1997, Gib takes more than marriage
vows in **TEXAS BABY,** Special Edition's
That's My Baby! title.
You won't be able to resist
Joan Elliott Pickart's **TEXAS BABY.**

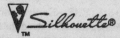

Silhouette

SPECIAL EDITION

TM

WELCOME TO SILVER CREEK COUNTY

A place full of small-town Texas charm, where
everybody knows your name and falling
in love is all in a day's work!

Award-winning author **SHARON DE VITA** has
spun several delightful stories full of matchmaking
kids, lonely lawmen, single parents and humorous
townsfolk! Watch for the first two books,
THE LONE RANGER
(Special Edition #1078, 1/97)
and
THE LADY AND THE SHERIFF
(Special Edition #1103, 5/97).
And there are many more heartwarming
tales to come!

So come on down to Silver Creek and make
a few friends—you'll be glad you did!

In February, Silhouette Books is proud
to present the sweeping, sensual new novel
by bestselling author

CAIT LONDON

about her unforgettable family—*The Tallchiefs*.

Everyone in Amen Flats, Wyoming, was talking about
Elspeth Tallchief. How she wasn't a thirty-three-year-old
virgin, after all. How she'd been keeping herself warm at
night all these years with a couple of secrets. And now one
of those secrets had walked right into town, sending
everyone into a frenzy. But Elspeth knew he'd come for
the *other* secret....

"Cait London is an irresistible storyteller…"
—*Romantic Times*

Don't miss TALLCHIEF FOR KEEPS by Cait London, available
at your favorite retail outlet in February from

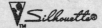

CLST

At last the wait is over...
In March
New York Times bestselling author

NORA ROBERTS

will bring us the latest from the Stanislaskis as
Natasha's now very grown-up stepdaughter,
Freddie, and Rachel's very sexy brother-in-law
Nick discover that love is worth waiting for in

WAITING FOR NICK

Silhouette Special Edition #1088

and in April
visit Natasha and Rachel again—or meet them
for the first time—in

The Stanislaski Sisters

containing TAMING NATASHA
and FALLING FOR RACHEL

Available wherever Silhouette books are sold.

Silhouette®